The Devil at Prayers

Queen And Country

Book 1

By Ellora Lawhorn

© Copyright 2024
Ellora Lawhorn

The right of Ellora Lawhorn to be identified as the author of this work has been asserted by her in accordance with the Copyright, Designs and Patents Act 1998.

All rights reserved. No reproduction, copy or transmission of this publication may be made without express prior written permission. No paragraph of this publication may be reproduced, copied or transmitted except with express prior written permission or in accordance with the provisions of the Copyright Act 1956 (as amended). Any person who commits any unauthorised act in relation to this publication may be liable to criminal prosecution and civil claims for damage.

All characters appearing in this work are fictitious. Any resemblance to real persons, living or dead, is purely coincidental. The opinions expressed herein are those of the author and not of MX Publishing.

Paperback ISBN 978-1-80424-375-6
ePub ISBN 978-1-80424-376-3
PDF ISBN 978-1-80424-377-0

Published by Orange Pip Books
An imprint of MX Publishing
335 Princess Park Manor, Royal Drive,
London, N11 3GX
www.mxpublishing.com

Cover design by Nusrat Abbas Awan

Chapter 1: True and False	3
Chapter 2: Characteristics of a Vigorous Mind	11
Chapter 3: Without a Single Doubt	19
Chapter 4: Danger Lurks Within	29
Chapter 5: The Soul of the Plot	37
Chapter 6: To Guard the Guards	43
Chapter 7: One Braver Thing	51
Chapter 8: A Populous and Smoky City	59
Chapter 9: No Longer Peace	67
Chapter 10: Profound Secret and Mystery	77
Chapter 11: Cunning Sin	85
Chapter 12: Power in Trust	97
Chapter 13: Be Bold	107
Chapter 14: The Art of War	117
Chapter 15: The Spider and the Fly	127
Chapter 16: Come Like Shadows	141
Chapter 17: Where Laws End	151
Chapter 18: Best Laid Schemes	161
Chapter 19: The Play's the Thing	171
Chapter 20: Love is Then Our Duty	183
Three Days Later	191

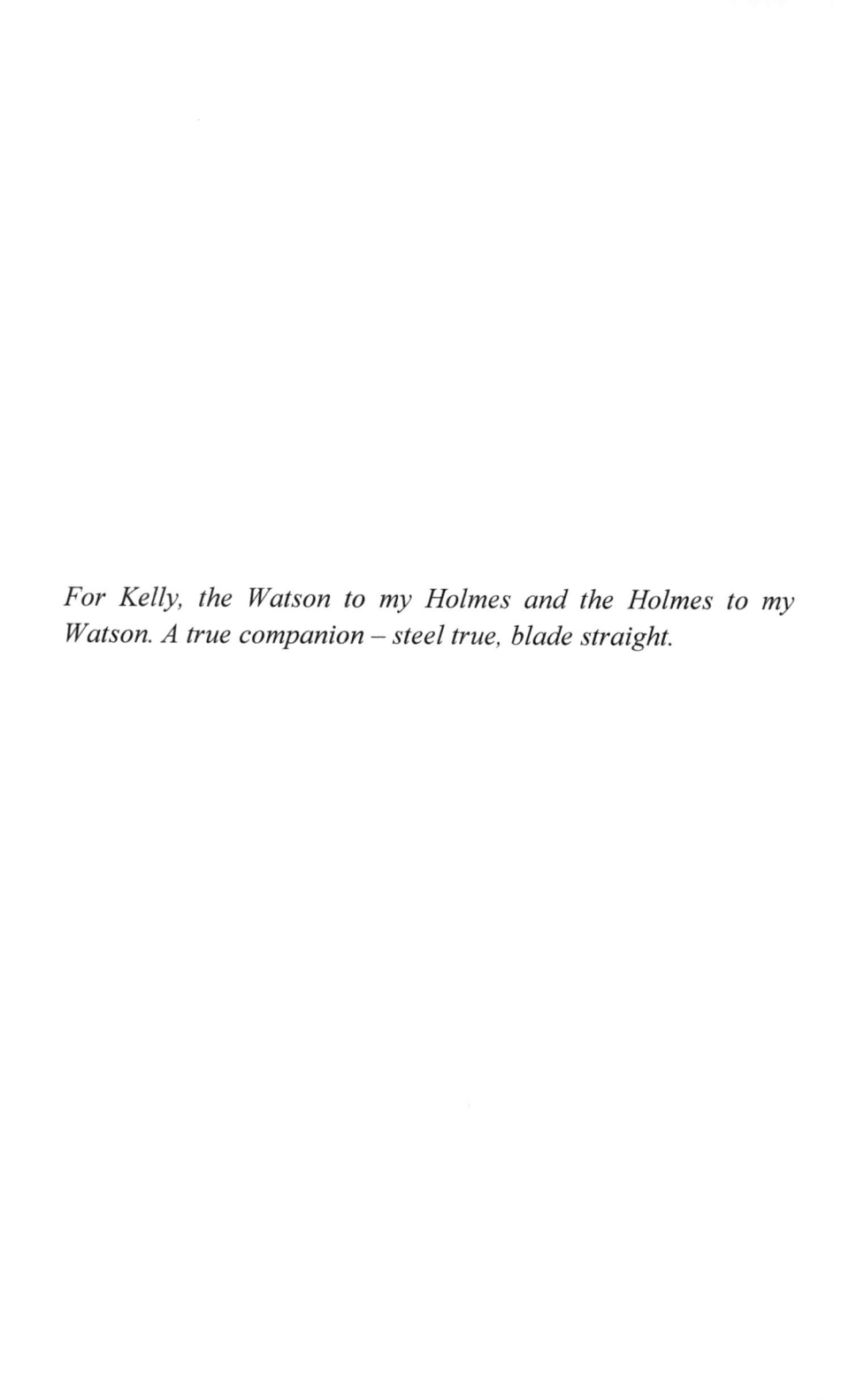

For Kelly, the Watson to my Holmes and the Holmes to my Watson. A true companion – steel true, blade straight.

'I don't want none of these sea-lawyers in the cabin a-coming home, unlooked for, like the devil at prayers.'
  – Robert Louis Stevenson, Treasure Island

Music for Readers of *The Devil at Prayers*

Southampton by Adam Young
Scotland by Paul Leonard-Morgan / BBC Scottish Symphony Orchestra
Spirit of the Gael by Alasdair Fraser
Lily's Theme by Alexandre Desplat
Davy Jones by Hans Zimmer
The Game is Afoot by Eternal Eclipse
Fog Bound by Klaus Badelt

A larger playlist by Ellora Lawhorn titled *Queen & Country* can be found on both Spotify and Apple Music, with some variations based on song availability. Ellora's profiles on both streaming platforms are also host to a number of *Q&C* inspired playlists based on book, character, and theme.

A Note to The Reader

    My grandmother died recently, leaving behind a small house in the Sussex countryside full of over 90 years worth of belongings for us to sort through.
    Constance lived a very full and exciting life. She was, in fact, one of the very first women detectives employed by Scotland Yard. She served as an intelligence agent during the prime of her life in the Second World War. Her life was full of decades worth of poignant and heart-pounding stories, which she loved to tell even when her memory began to fail.
    Besides her own tales, there were those of her mother. I'm sure you've all heard of (and perhaps read) Sherlock Holmes's adventures, published most discreetly by Doctor John Watson's editor, Sir Arthur Conan Doyle. They haven't lost their popularity over the last century; in fact, they have inspired an ever-growing

number of books, shows, and movies. But the stories left out an important detail: Constance's mother, Emily.

I assume that Doctor Watson never mentioned his half-sister because it would have caused a public uproar at the time. Indeed, I know of a great many other details he fudged in his narratives for various reasons, whether they be personal or political.

Emily was, in fact, a very real figure in the Sherlockian lore. Despite her absence being a product of fear from societal judgement at the time, the woman kept her own extended accounts of some cases she had the privilege of experiencing with the famous duo. They appear to centre on a far darker, bloodier truth than the light-hearted, family-friendly tales Doyle approved for publication. Most of them remain as yet unrecorded by any other source.

It is these narratives that my brother and I uncovered in a steamer trunk in the attic while cleaning out Grandma Constance's house.

It's been long enough that these stories cannot harm anyone, and it is my belief that they will be widely appreciated and enjoyed. Emily's personal accounts do much to humanise these figures of long ago, and I do hope that you feel less alone after reading them.

To preserve their authenticity, I have not changed any British spellings or older expressions in these volumes. I do hope the modern reader may easily adapt to them.

However you choose to utilise these tales, I ask that you read them with wonder and respect for my great-grandmother's legacy.

Yours,
Renee Watson, 2019

Chapter 1: True and False

'He who would distinguish the true from the false must have an adequate idea of what is true and false.'
– Benedict Spinoza

The library's bay window was a loyal companion to the world beyond; it had never strayed from the same view since its installation. The panes formed a transparent, yet altogether immovable barrier between myself and the picturesque hills outside.

It wasn't that I couldn't step out the front door and break that barrier; not at all like I didn't have any freedom – I had enough, so long as it didn't take me far from home.

It would surprise most people how quickly being confined to an area of twenty miles becomes tedious. Thus, the library was my haven – one of few places on our sizable estate from which I was never running away. So many of these volumes could take me far and wide without ever leaving my favourite armchair.

This morning, I'd woken up with the same view out of my window, again yearning for something more.

As I stood in front of the window, I looked down at the book in my hand. *Treasure Island* was a recent publication by Robert Louis Stevenson. The printing date was less than five years ago. Father wouldn't have cared enough about the maturing interests of his children to include recent works of literary entertainment in the massive library had Mother not insisted that we procure a copy.

I took another glance at the lush, green hillsides before settling down into the armchair. The piece of furniture that had become an extension of me, like an arm or leg, was placed in front of the window but not directly facing it, so as to give the perfect angle and amount of light required for daytime reading.

It seemed an eccentric choice to call one's favourite, but it was the adventure that called to me. Inside these pages, I wasn't the stifled daughter of a mysterious and reclusive businessman. I was a thrill-seeker, an innkeeper, a pirate, a treasure hunter. I watched a parrot fly over my head and felt the salty breeze across my face. My frame was braced, balancing with the rocking of the ship, and the sand felt warm beneath my feet.

The closest I got to this in daily life was the newspaper's weekly summaries of notable crimes across Britain. There had been a fascinating report recently about an art theft from a Scottish museum that read like a story out of my favourite tales.

As I opened *Treasure Island* to the first chapter, I recalled the night Mother read it to us, shortly after Father had brought it back from a trip to London. She adopted the voices of the characters and helped us act out the scenes, my sister's fingers curled like a hook and myself with a tapered candle for a sword.

Not long after, Mother had grown too weary for any such expenditures of energy. And a month later, the nearby town's doctor informed us of her quickly deteriorating health.

I shook my head to dispel these thoughts. The past was done. Dwelling on it was far less satisfying than the story I held in my hands. I took a breath, focused my eyes, and began to read.

Squire Trelawney, Dr. Livesey, and the rest of these gentlemen having asked me to write down the whole particulars about Treasure Island, from the beginning to the end, keeping nothing back but the bearings of the island, and that only because there is still treasure not yet lifted, I take up my pen in the year of grace 17--, and go back to the time when my father kept the "Admiral Benbow" inn, and the brown old seaman, with the sabre cut, first took up his lodging under our roof...

My attention broke away from the page with the sound of echoing footsteps at the back of the library.

My shoulders tensed. A headache formed upon thinking that Mrs Thompson, head of the housekeeping staff, might be disturbing my peaceful reading to inform me that she was going to wash my curtains. She always insisted that I give her my permission to go forward with her tasks.

Instead, I heaved a sigh of relief when a more familiar, youthful voice called out, 'Emily!'

'I'm back here!'

The footsteps hastened. A few seconds later, a face appeared around the corner, identical to mine in every feature, flushed with excitement and urgency.

I arose, setting down the open book in my seat. 'Ariana, is everything all right?'

My twin sister grabbed my arm and pulled me behind one of the shelves. She spoke in a soft voice, as though someone was watching us, listening into a secretive conversation in the vacant room. 'Do we know any tall, respectably dressed professors who recently arrived from London?'

'None come to mind.' I narrowed my eyes. 'Why?'

'Father has a visitor. I was passing the dining hall as the staff showed him in. Father and he shook hands, seeming quite friendly.'

'Did you hear them discussing these particulars which you have used to describe this mysterious visitor?'

'No, but I did see some indications that proved them true.'

'Which are?'

'There is chalk residue between his right forefinger and thumb, betraying his occupation. I noticed it when he shook hands with Father.'

'But why a professor? Why not just a teacher?'

'He teaches college-level mathematics. His coat was hanging in the hall, and I found this in his pocket.' From behind her back, Ariana pulled a worn, wrinkled piece of paper.

I crossed my arms. 'You are telling me you went through an unfamiliar gentleman's pockets and actually *took* things?'

My sister shrugged. 'When Father has a "friendly" visitor all the way from London, wouldn't it be only hospitable to introduce him to his children? Besides, you'd have done the same.'

'Perhaps he is planning to introduce us.'

'We both know he wouldn't wait unless he had something to hide.'

Sighing, I snatched the paper.

Visiting lectures:

- *Cambridge*
- *Oxford*
- *Edinburgh*

Assignments to collect:
- *Darcy*
- *Phillips*
- *Teller*
- *Kelley*

Ariana grabbed it, flipping it over. 'Wrong side.'

I raised my eyebrows, but said nothing. The formula on the opposite side of the paper was not one I was familiar with, but fortunately, it was labelled.

The Binomial Theorem as presented by Sir Isaac Newton:
$(a+b)^5 = a^5 + 5a^4b + 10a^3b^2 + 10a^2b^3 + 5ab^4 + b$

I cleared my throat. 'So far I follow, but what about this gentleman being recently arrived from London?'

'This was also in his coat pocket.' My twin pulled out two more slips of paper.

Train tickets, the stamped first half of a round trip. Victoria Station to Cambridge, Suffolk, and Thorndon Station. Dated 12th August, 1887.

Today.

'I see. You do not think this visit is what it seems to be.'

Ariana fixed me with a look. 'Nothing has been as it seems with Father ever since…'

I nodded. 'Then how do we "accidentally" get introduced to this mysterious professor?'

'I already thought of that. We'll walk into the dining hall, "unaware" that Father has a guest, and ask to take our horses out for a little exercise.'

'How do we know that we can find him there?'

'Mrs Thompson.'

The plan seemed plausible enough. We shook hands, an unspoken oath only made between twins.

After a short detour for Ariana to return the stolen items to the stranger's coat, we stepped through the large double doors and into the dining room.

'Father,' I spoke right away, 'could Ariana and I take out the horses for a ride? We'd be home by dinner, of course, and stay– Oh, I'm terribly sorry, I did not realise you had a visitor.'

I allowed my gaze to fall on the guest, who stood across the table from my father.

Just as Ariana had said, he was tall, much taller than Father. His forehead was domed. His dark eyes were deeply sunken, staring out at the world with an extraordinary keenness. The professor's whole head was engaged in some constant oscillation, almost as a cobra, poised to strike, and yet those glassy, dark eyes remained fixed immovably on my sister and I.

His shoulders were rounded, presumably from bending over a desk frequently. There were wrinkles around his mouth and he sported a receding hairline, but I had a sneaking suspicion that these were not due to age, but experience.

My eyes fell on the chalk residue on his right hand.

'Ah.' Father's brow crinkled as he turned to his guest. 'James, these are my daughters. Emily, Ariana, this is an old acquaintance of mine, Mr Moriarty.'

The man's mouth turned upwards in a smile of rather dubious pretence. I did not sense any emotion or happiness behind it.

'A pleasure, ladies.' He bowed.

'James and I were business partners long ago. He found himself not far away from our humble estate and decided to pay me a visit.'

James gestured with outspread arms. 'I wouldn't want to keep either of you from your ride. I'll be staying for dinner, so there will be plenty of time to converse then, I am sure.'

With consent from Father, the two of us left the dining room. Once the heavy wooden doors were closed, Ariana turned to me.

'Father doesn't have business partners. And you saw that train ticket; he was deliberately headed for Thorndon.'

I took a deep breath as if to brace my body for what my mind already knew. 'Father's lying to us.'

Chapter 2: Characteristics of a Vigorous Mind

'Curiosity is one of the permanent and certain characteristics of a vigorous mind.'
– Samuel Johnson

I poked my head into the back room of the stables where the elderly stable hand could usually be found whittling.

'Gus?'

Besides the wood shavings on the floor, the room was devoid of tangible presence. I shrugged lightly, hanging up my riding gloves. The right one dropped to the ground as a voice came from behind me.

'I saw the two of you returning and wanted a word with you.'

Professor Moriarty leaned comfortably against the wall, fingering something inside his pocket. As he pulled it halfway out, I saw it was an advertisement for some new art exhibit.

'I hope it was not a requirement for Ariana to be present, as she has already returned to the house.' I kept my voice measured, hoping to make it clear that I did not like the looks of him.

The man waved a hand in dismissal. 'I can speak to her later. But right now...' He trailed off, cocking his head at me.

'Why must you speak to me alone?'

'I would like to tell you that you put on a very good show this afternoon, pretending you did not realise I was there as an excuse to be introduced.'

I froze in the act of buttoning my left shoe. 'Was it honestly that obvious?'

Moriarty smirked. 'Apparently not to your father.'

'Is that all?' I snatched my hat from the peg and held it expectantly. 'Or are you about to reveal to me how you knew I was pretending?'

His dark eyes languidly travelled to all corners of the stable, but he fixed them again on me, monitoring my body language. 'Your sister went through my coat pockets.'

'And she undoubtedly told me of your arrival.'

He nodded, but said nothing.

I decided to continue, taking a step closer to him. He showed no reaction.

'You are a professor of mathematics. But you are not here on a friendly visit or to speak to Father of formulas and numbers.'

'Pray continue.'

'The train tickets show where you were *planning* to go. You weren't simply riding *by* Thorndon. Your visit here was very much deliberate.'

'I see nothing wrong with my actions.'

When I next spoke, I was surprised to hear how cold my tone had become. 'There is the fact that you did not bother to correct my father when he said your decision was spur of the moment.' I jammed my hat onto my head with alarming force. 'You would, I think, find it a good idea to inform him of the real reason for your visit, whatever that might be.'

Moriarty produced another smirk, devoid of any emotion resembling humour. 'Your father knows very well the reason I am here. I thought we had established that *he* lied to you and your sister.'

I paused near the doorway.

'So I was correct.'

'Tell your sister,' called Moriarty as I left the stables, 'that she really should stop snooping. It might get her into a lot of trouble one day.'

I felt his eyes on me as I stiffly began to follow the familiar stone path, repressing a shiver. My clammy hands gripped the front of my dress tightly as I struggled to control my posture.

The foyer was empty as I walked in. Where could Ariana have gone?

However, I decided not to look for her. I did not want to enrage her with an account of my conversation with that despicable man until I knew more.

Struck again by how unnerved he had made me, my body trembled with a violent shudder.

I bolted to the window. The pathway, and indeed the entire lawn, were empty. Was he still out there in the stable? He must be, unless he had taken the back door and gone out towards the woods.

The urge to march back out there was overwhelming. This man simply could not go off alone on our property.

I stilled my hand on the doorknob. The last thing I needed was for Moriarty to know how he had affected me.

Exhaling deeply, I walked deliberately towards the library.

I bit my lip as I entered the cool room, listening carefully for any indications of my twin sister's presence. I called her name after easing the door behind me, just to be certain.

Satisfied with my unanswered query, I passed a half dozen thick and fully laden shelves on my way to the alcove I was seeking. An ebony book stand housed the thickest volume I had ever seen: a *Who's Who* compendium of each prominent family's lineage in all the British Isles.

As a young child, too small to reach the top of the stand, I had only been allowed to view it as my mother held me up to gaze with wonder upon the crisp, thin pages inked delicately and updated with each census.

Even now, I approached the tome with a sort of reverence, holding my breath as the spine cracked and the contents were revealed to me. I scanned through the sacred pages for the letter M.

Skimming through Marshes and Maypoles and Morgans, I finally reached Moriarty.

I glanced behind me just in case.

Dinner had been a rather quiet affair until Father and the professor broke out of their conversation.

'James and I have some business matters to settle,' he turned to us, 'so I hope you girls wouldn't mind terribly if he occupied a guest room for a couple of nights.'

Ariana and I froze.

Moriarty looked at us, then at Father. 'If this will be a complication, Peter, I will be more than willing to procure a room in town.'

'That won't be necessary, James. My daughters will just need to adapt to a small, temporary adjustment in their lives.'

I managed to keep a calm outward demeanour, but I could feel Ariana's fist clenching in her lap.

We've made larger adjustments before. Like losing our mother. Like hardly being allowed off the grounds.

The two of us spent the rest of the meal sitting in silence. Immediately as we were excused, to allow the two men to speak alone, we were up and out the door in seconds.

'I don't like him.' Ariana's voice was flat. 'Father's never been forthcoming, but he's never lied through his teeth like this!'

'Prepare to like him even less.' I proceeded to relay the events of my conversation with Moriarty, and his final warning.

My sister had been hugging her knees to her chest, rocking back and forth on my bed. When I finished, she leaped up and paced angrily to the window, muttering a barely audible string of Latin insults and curses. Her eyes were filled with rage as she turned back to me.

'What in the name of Bloody Mary does Father think he's doing? Can't he see past that façade?'

'I don't know, Ariana.'

She, however, didn't seem to hear me, for she obliviously continued her rant.

'Ariana!'

She stopped, drawing a breath. She released the chair she'd been holding in a grip so tight I was afraid it would break.

'I realise that is excellent Latin practice, but please, keep yourself in check.'

Her eyes were still blazing, but she bit her lip and nodded.

I rose from my desk chair. 'All right. We need to find out more about this man. What do you propose we do?'

Ariana's eyes had been fixed on the ground, but when her gaze met mine, it held a devious glint. 'They're both downstairs, playing billiards.'

I nodded, a smirk rising nearly to the surface. 'To the professor's room, it is.'

Ariana shook her head. 'Somehow, he knew I'd gone through his pockets. He'd surely realise immediately if we'd been in his room.'

'So, we'll have to turn our search to Father's study.'

'They obviously do know each other quite well, so Father must have something informative on him.'

As we stole down the staircase barely a moment later, I whispered, 'I can tell you one other thing about this professor.'

'And what's that?'

'I did some looking today. His surname is Irish. It means "warrior of the sea."'

'So, he's Poseidon on land.'

'The Moriarty family are also old Suffolk nobility.'

Two steps ahead of me, my sister abruptly stopped. '*Where* in Suffolk?'

'Earl Soham.'

'That's disturbingly close to here.'

Ariana was right – it was hardly even twenty miles. I swallowed.

'Let's focus on sleuthing without being caught for now.'

I didn't say what I was thinking: Ariana and I had never been allowed twenty miles from home. It seemed more than probable that we had been kept from approaching Earl Soham and the Moriarty family estate. But was it twenty miles all around rather than just Earl Soham? But I couldn't help thinking it was the latter, even if Father had not specified. Because only specifying the town would indicate a place or certain people that he wanted us to avoid, and not just a concern for our safety. We would be sure to question it and express a desire to visit there even more.

But what could be so horrible about the Moriarty family estate that we would be forbidden from even approaching the town?

'Aren't you coming?' Ariana pulled me out of my stupor.

I nodded silently, still preoccupied with my thoughts.

It wasn't long before we reached the first-floor hallway where Father kept his study. I paused outside the door for a moment to stare at the name painstakingly engraved into the wooden door:

Sir Peter Ashford, Esq.

I pressed my ear to the wood. No sounds came from within.

'I told you they were in the billiards room!' hissed Ariana.

'Shhh, that's still just down the hall!'

She held up her hands in surrender as I opened the door noiselessly.

We slipped in. As soon as Ariana had eased the door shut, I lit the gas lamps dimly. I crossed to his desk while she knelt by one of the large boxes of old papers in the corner.

Opening one of the top drawers, I happened to look up at the desk's surface. My eyes immediately fell on a piece of paper filled with my father's cramped handwriting, the name *Moriarty* visible at the top.

'Ariana...'

My sister replaced a stack of files in the box and came to stand by me as I gently picked up the paper, skimming paragraphs about the man's childhood and early career. There were several hastily scribbled lines at the bottom, punctuated by a splash of spilled ink in the left corner:

Currently holds a chair as professor of mathematics at the University of St. Andrews, Scotland. Possesses all the hereditary genius of our family.

Ariana gasped. '*Our* family? But could that mean...'

Her eyes met mine, and in her gaze I read the unfinished question.

Were Moriarty and my father *related?*

I took a shaky breath, trying to shed the feeling that I was on the verge of something huge. I took another breath and moved to the final line, underlined thickly several times:

Caution advised. Knows the family secret.

'What on earth is the "family secret?"'

I cast a nervous glance at the door. 'Well, I certainly know what it must have to do with. It's overshadowed us all our lives.'

'What's that?'

'The fact that you and I are Watsons, not Ashfords.'

Chapter 3: Without a Single Doubt

> 'The first precept was never to accept a thing as true until I knew it as such without a single doubt.'
> – Rene Descartes

The next morning, I awoke to a terrible screeching sound aimed directly into my ear.

My first instinct was to thrust one hand over my wounded ear as quickly as possible, using the other to massage my frontal lobe.

Finally, my eyes flickered open to the sight of my sister, holding my violin within three inches of my ear.

I winced, wondering how much permanent damage it would cause to be woken up by the sound of an inexperienced violinist far too close to your face.

'Ariana, now do you understand why I warned you never to play that instrument unless I give you my consent? Or violin lessons? Honestly, you really are much more suited for the piano.'

My sister dropped the instrument onto a nearby chair in relief. 'You needed to be woken up somehow. If I shake you, you flail.'

When I looked behind my sister and out my bedroom window, I saw the horizon just beginning to tinge itself a gentle shade of coral.

'Honestly, Ariana! *The sun is still rising!*'

She didn't even afford a glance behind her. 'Yes, I know it's early, but it's an urgent matter!'

As I pushed myself up in bed, I realised that my sister was already fully dressed.

'How long have you been up?'

She looked at me seriously. 'Honestly, Emily, do you believe I could have gone to sleep last night, with that man sleeping down the hall? I'm awfully surprised you managed it.'

'What is the urgent matter?' I asked my identical twin, wishing that *identical* meant I could read her thoughts.

She started as though the memory of her intentions had slapped her in the face, and reached beside her, picking up a slip of paper.

On seeing the familiar, angular handwriting, I uttered a curse. 'That's his handwriting.'

'He slipped it under the door an hour ago. I was itching to wake you up sooner. Before you read the note, do you have any other observations and deductions to make?'

I studied the writing on the page. I studied the small blotch of ink in the corner. I studied the paper itself.

After a few seconds, another piece of the puzzle fell into place.

'It's not a particular stationery.'

She smiled. 'Exactly. Now explain why that's strange.'

That was just like Ariana, always testing, making sure we were on the same page.

'Well, we know from last night that he was a professor of mathematics at the University of St. Andrews.'

And that was it. Key word: *was.*

'If he was still a professor, he would be writing on the University's stationery. He would carry it everywhere for official correspondence.'

The paper was not the thick cardstock used for stationery. There was no monogram on it and the watermark was the familiar jester's cap that had engendered the name: foolscap.

Ariana smiled, her eyes glinting in the early morning sunlight. '*Precisely.* The only reason he would no longer be using the school's stationery is—'

'That he no longer works there.'

This was one of the more triumphant instances where Ariana's thoughts *were* plain enough for me to finish her sentences.

She nodded, but stayed silent, and I used that as an indicator to continue reading the note:

My dear girls,

Going through my pockets was rather a mistake, but last night was a very close call. It is fortunate for you that I did not decide to inform Peter that you two were in his study.

I am inclined to give you a piece of advice, if you insist upon snooping: do remember to shut off the lamps before leaving a room.

You already know that Peter and I are related. You know there is a family secret. There must be some sort of connection between the two, mustn't there? I urge you to think, but if that is too much of a challenge for you, I shall be in the Northwest Passage at noon.

And remember that nothing is as it seems.

'Too much of a challenge for us!' I spat out. 'Ariana, do you realise how much he's underestimated us?'

She nodded, slower this time, more thoughtfully. 'I know we are capable of thinking this through, Emily, but he's *offering us the truth.* We'd be fools not to take him up on that offer.'

I got out of bed as she spoke, mulling over her words as my feet hit the floor. She made an excellent point: we might be intelligent, but there was no competing with this man. There were many words that could be used to paint a mental picture of Moriarty, and *genius* was prominent among them.

As I stood at the window, watching the sun slowly rise over the hills, my sister began speaking again.

'There's still something about him I don't trust. I can't really put my finger on it, but…'

That was when I *did* put my finger on it.

The newspaper from last week. That small paragraph about the Scottish museum robbery. The pamphlet in Moriarty's pocket yesterday afternoon.

I whirled around to face my sister. 'Do you remember that small article in the papers last Wednesday?'

It only took her a moment to recall any "small articles" the two of us would have discussed together and narrow down the possibilities.

'The painting reported stolen from the Museum at the University of Saint Andrews?'

'*Yes.* A teacher at the University was suspected of stealing the painting, based on an anonymous tip to the Dean. To avoid scandal, the suspect was merely asked to resign his post. And when Father introduced us, he said *Mr* Moriarty. Not Professor.'

Even as I began to speak, Ariana's eyes widened, and her lips parted slightly in comprehension. But I held up my hand to signify that I was not finished.

'Yesterday, when Moriarty came to speak to me in the stables, I happened to observe a pamphlet sticking out of his pocket. It was from the museum, dated Monday last, advertising a formal reception for the unveiling of a new painting which the museum had acquired.'

'*Shipwreck in Stormy Seas,* by Claude Joseph Vernet.'

I nodded. 'Of course he received an automatic invitation to the unveiling, as a professor at the University. He realised this was a monumental opportunity…'

'…and took it,' finished Ariana. 'But, why steal it in the first place? And why *that* painting in particular?'

My eyes glinted. 'That's what we'll find out at noon.'

At breakfast, Moriarty and my father were, once more, having a deeply involved conversation in quiet tones.

Ariana and I sat next to each other, observing the men's body language, straining our ears to hear some part of their conversation.

Finally, I caught the last half of Moriarty's statement:

'…and that was when you deserted us. Think of this as your chance for redemption, Peter.'

My head turned to give Ariana a sideways glance. Her eyes met mine in understanding.

After a few more moments, the men's conversation grew into more normal tones, and I could hear Moriarty's voice clearly.

'I was thinking of taking an excursion this afternoon. That covered pathway off the northwestern side of the courtyard seems like an excellent spot for solitary reflection on nature.'

The Northwest Passage. Of course, the note hadn't meant the trade route that Hernán Cortés had commissioned Francisco de Ulloa to locate in 1539, it had meant the passage on the northwestern side of our estate.

'Luncheon will be served at one-thirty, am I correct?'

My father nodded.

'Then I believe I shall make my way over there about noon.'

A few moments later, Ariana and I were headed towards the doors when Moriarty spoke again.

'Peter, I believe your daughters have a rather unsafe measure of curiosity. It would be in your best interest to rein them in.'

As he spoke, I could feel a prickly feeling on the back of my neck. From the way Ariana stiffened beside me, I knew that she felt it too.

Exactly five minutes to noon found us entering the courtyard, facing the familiar stone walkways and benches placed between well-trimmed shrubs.

We walked straight across it to the northwest corner, through a doorway into a covered stone passage. Carved columns supported the roof, creating open windows bordered on each side and a railing at the bottom.

Immediately our eyes fell upon a tall, slim figure standing about halfway down the path, staring out a window at the infamous Suffolk hills.

Without turning around or, indeed, moving at all, he spoke: 'You are two minutes and twenty-seven seconds early, girls.'

The two of us came to stand beside Moriarty. We saw that snake-like face, those small, dark spheres, the pestilential outlook of his mind.

'I was certain you would come. You are just too inquisitive to let the offer go to waste.'

'We know that you are no longer a professor at the University of St. Andrews.'

'*And* we know *why,*' added Ariana.

Moriarty's thin eyebrows arched in surprise, rising high into the domain of his overhanging forehead. 'My, you can put two and two together even better than I thought. So I take it you read about the robbery in the papers last Wednesday?'

'I'd really like to know who submitted that anonymous tip.'

'There was no trail left, no uproar. No vitality to the whole affair. It was all too dull.'

'You did it,' Ariana breathed. 'But why? And what is so significant about that painting?'

Moriarty afforded a small smile. 'You see, I have rather a fascination with fine artwork. About a year ago, I acquired a Jean Baptiste Greuze – quite a desirable piece, in my opinion. When I was under suspicion for stealing that Vernet from the University museum, they thought I had stolen the Greuze as well.' He ended the statement as if such a presumption were scandalous.

Ariana and I merely traded dubious glances.

'A fascination with fine artwork is not sufficient motive, *Mr* Moriarty,' I told him. 'When you attended that unveiling last week, you seized your opportunity almost as soon as you knew the particulars of the artist who put it down on canvas, almost as if you were waiting for the perfect piece of art to arrive.'

After a moment's hesitation during which he carefully picked out his words, he started to speak. 'There is a man whose success I have been following for some time. He has much more talent than any of the professionals, yet he calls himself an amateur. I believe his chosen term for it is a *private consulting detective*. When the police find themselves with a case beyond their limits, they bring it to Sherlock Holmes, the remarkable reasoner, who can often bring cases to a close without ever leaving the comfort of his sitting room.

'Mr Holmes is of French descent, and Claude Joseph Vernet was one of Holmes' ancestors. His grandson, Emile Jean Horace Vernet, was Holmes' great-uncle. I hoped this might attract the man's attention. And now, I am free to move all my affairs back to London to plan for greater things.'

Something seemed very wrong. This man was calmly and willingly confessing to us that he had stolen a prized 18th-century painting hardly a week ago.

I could read the same thought on Ariana's face, but we both decided to keep gathering more information, as long as we were there.

'That connection you mentioned... What was it?'

'So you remembered that, did you? I may not be as old as you think, but your father is also not as young as he appears.'

'Brothers.' I spoke the word at the same moment as it entered my mind. 'You're brothers, aren't you?'

He smiled and nodded, again as if complimenting our understanding. 'Very good, Miss *Watson.*'

Some relief crawled in to sit beside the utter shock. He *wasn't* our uncle. We were not Ashfords, not Moriartys.

'Why did Father change his name?'

'Can we just say that our family, despite being nobility, has a rather... questionable history. My brother wanted no more to do with us. So he legally changed his name and began a new life with a woman who already had two young daughters.'

My mother had previously been married to someone named Watson. When Ariana and I were infants, she remarried this *Ashford* while her children kept their biological father's surname.

When we asked why we were not Ashfords, Mother had never said a word. The look in her eyes betrayed it all: it was dangerous to be an Ashford.

Not that being Watsons had let us off without sufficient scandal.

My sister spoke again, her voice far steadier than I felt. 'But why are you telling us this?'

Moriarty answered calmly and easily, 'Because you did not heed my warning about what happens to curious cats. Now, when you realise that the truth comes with a price, you will know you only have yourselves to blame.'

Chapter 4: Danger Lurks Within

> *'For many men that stumble at the threshold*
> *Are well foretold that danger lurks within.'*
> *– William Shakespeare*

'I can't believe this.' After luncheon, *deja vu* struck as my sister angrily paced my bedroom floor. 'Can't we go to Father?'

I sighed, setting down my pen and the empty paper. 'Father lied to us, Ariana, how can we trust him?'

She thrust her hand at me emphatically. 'That's precisely the problem! He lied to protect the "family secret," but we never even found out what that is!'

I massaged my temple with one hand. There were still things we didn't know, but evidently, we already knew more than was safe. Former professor Moriarty had threatened us, undeniably.

'You did not heed my warning...'
'The truth comes at a price...'
'You have only yourselves to blame...'

I closed my eyes. Barely a moment later, I remembered this morning. 'Ariana, what about that bit of their conversation we overheard at breakfast?'

'And that was when you deserted us. Think of this as your chance for redemption, Peter!'

She snapped her fingers. 'Yes, what does "chance for redemption" mean?'

I groaned and stood up, nearly getting knocked over as my twin swept past me.

A million thoughts ran through my head. The whole thing was a tangled skein of yarn; I needed my mind clear to try and make sense of it.

We knew that my father had estranged himself from the Moriarty family, even going so far as to change his name. And it was certain that Moriarty had come here, to his brother, because of his resignation from the University. What could this man want with my father and why was he lying to us about it? He was obviously trying to hide the fact that the two of them were brothers. But why? And what motive did Moriarty have for not telling him what we knew?

It took me a moment to notice that Ariana had stopped, stock still, facing the door.

'What is it?'

And then I saw it, slipped under the door. It couldn't have been placed more than a minute ago.

I swore under my breath, rushing over to retrieve the piece of paper, while Ariana stood pale and stiff. I fumbled to unfold the note. I was not shocked to discover the thin, slanted script belonging to ex-professor James Moriarty:

I offered redemption. A chance for him to help a family member in need. When he hears of my offer, I am sure he will not refuse.

I tilted the paper at an angle, and the black liquid glimmered.

'The ink is still fresh. He must have been outside the door.'

But Ariana hardly reacted. I wondered if she had even heard me.

'Emily, we already know the family secret.'

I stopped.

Did we?

We knew that Ariana and I were not our Father's biological children. We knew that Mother had been married to someone named Watson, and that he had likely died when we were infants. Then she remarried. But was there more to it?

Evidently, Ariana was thinking the same. 'What more could there be?'

There were only so many things that could be added to the situation, and none of them fit. Unless we had missed something entirely, then we knew all there was to know.

I met Ariana's gaze.

But what was so secret about a second marriage?

Unless it wasn't about our direct lineage at all. Unless it was about Father's family. It could be the reason he had distanced himself from them, then taken every precaution to make sure we avoided them like the plague.

So what did they want from him now? And, perhaps most ominously, what was Moriarty planning to do if our father refused?

'Are you sure you don't want my help?'

Ariana half-smiled at me from her position in the doorway of the library. 'Are you sure *you* don't want *my* help? It *is* reconnaissance, Em. You should have a partner.'

'I will be fine. If suspected, there is always the option to retreat and later deny. You, on the other hand, are taking the overwhelming job of a one-person research team.'

'I can manage, dear sister. Now go!' She shooed me away with a wave of her arm. Once I turned to leave, she softly shut the library door to commence her search for any information on the history of the Moriartys. The *Who's Who* entry was astonishingly short. Almost as though purposefully kept vague.

I, on the other hand, headed down the hall to Father's study where I knew the two men were engaging in *"business."* We had figured the best plan was to listen through the door and act nonchalant if one of them happened to come out.

I paused to wipe my sweaty hands on my skirts. Then I leaned my ear close to the wooden barricade.

'...regret it, I am *quite* sure!'

What followed was a heavy sigh. 'Leanne would never have approved of this. She never did. Said the whole lot of you were despicable, and she was right.'

Then there was a harsh laugh. 'Leanne is *dead!*'

I heard a loud bang as something hit the wooden surface of the desk.

'And by heaven, I'll swear it was your doing!'

'I had nothing against your wife.' The tone was almost taunting.

'You hated her!'

'Tut, tut, Peter. This is precisely why we cast you off. You cannot hold your temper, unlike the rest of the family.'

'That is because you don't have hearts,' snarled my father.

'Don't you mean *we,* Peter? You *are* one of us.'

'Don't be a fool. I never belonged in that family and you all knew it. How could I ever bear the disgrace of that surname? Live, knowing that anywhere I went, I would bear the mark of such a cold-blooded clan.'

'Leanne would've encouraged you to embrace the challenge. It builds character. She was all about character, wasn't she?'

'If only you hadn't killed her, James.'

'I had nothing to do with your wife's death, Peter. It was consumption, wasn't it?'

'That's only what the doctor said.'

Moriarty elicited a low chuckle. 'So you do not trust the judgement of a worthy physician?'

'Why did you kill her?'

'She may have threatened me, but I am certainly not responsible for her death.'

My father let out a high laugh, a clear mark of near-hysteria. 'You were always the best actor among us, James. How can I know you aren't bluffing?'

'Because having blood on my hands – figuratively, of course – would only tarnish my reputation and ruin my chances of staying out of prison. I'm here because I'm desperate enough as it is.'

'Even if it wasn't you directly, you could have had her killed. You can still be held accountable.'

'Oh, please, Peter. You know such an emotional accusation would never even make it to the courtroom.'

I could only picture the smirk on Moriarty's face.

He continued, 'You're clearly just unable to cope with the unexpected loss. You still live in seclusion, even from your own daughters. They just remind you too much of your beloved Leanne, don't they?'

'I only distance myself from them so I can find a way to keep them away from all of you.'

'Family always comes knocking, Peter.'

'I should have just slammed the door,' Father muttered.

'I shall be back presently,' Moriarty said. 'I must retrieve a document from my chambers. Then we may resume negotiations.'

I quickly walked down the hall as if I hadn't just overheard my father accusing his own brother of killing my mother.

The door opened and our unwanted visitor called out, 'Would you mind opening the window? It feels terribly stuffy in there.'

I heard the latch click and a soft voice spoke near my ear. 'Shall we go into the library, Miss Watson? I believe that is where we shall find your sister.'

'How did you know—'

'Come along now, I mustn't leave your father very long.'

I took a breath to steady myself – for I was slightly frightened – and began walking towards the library.

Moriarty's footsteps were right behind me, slow and deliberate.

We entered the library where Ariana immediately looked up from a pile of books and froze.

I vaguely heard Moriarty shutting the door behind us. He clapped his hands together.

'Sit down, girls.'

Wavering like the last autumn leaf clinging to a bare December tree, my sister sat down. I took the chair beside her.

On the other side of the table, Moriarty faced us with his arms crossed. 'Miss Ariana, have you found anything interesting?'

She just stared at him levelly.

That surely meant she'd found something. I wanted to meet her gaze, but I didn't dare. Not when he was so perceptive.

Moriarty turned his gaze to me. 'Do you think I am lying, Miss Emily?'

'I do think it is true that you wouldn't want my mother's blood directly on your hands.'

Ariana's mouth fell open in abject horror. 'He *killed our mother?*'

'No,' I said icily, 'he merely had her killed. To that, he practically confessed.'

My sister rose from her seat, but Moriarty held up a hand. 'Leanne Watson-Ashford threatened me. She had some information she could not be trusted to keep. I was only tying up loose ends.'

I spoke despite the lump in my throat. 'And your offer of Father's chance for redemption?'

'He refused.'

At that moment, Mrs Thompson let out a scream.

My heart froze.

Beside me, it was as if Ariana had ceased breathing. Moriarty merely blinked at us. 'As I said. Loose ends.'

Chapter 5: The Soul of the Plot

'*And much of Madness, and more of Sin, and Horror the soul of the plot.*'
– *Edgar Allan Poe*

We sat still as stone in our seats, not daring to move.

'You've killed both our parents,' Ariana finally whispered.

Moriarty chuckled, his arms remaining crossed calmly. 'No. Miss Emily can attest that Peter Ashford was alive and well when I left his study. I simply cannot have done anything to him myself.'

Ariana swore in French. Whatever the language – French, Greek, Latin, or Gaelic – I wholly agreed with my sister.

But the professor was right as well. Being shut in the library, standing directly in front of us, gave him an undeniable alibi. I knew that he was the one ultimately behind my father's murder, but he couldn't be held accountable in the eyes of the law.

Moriarty raised his eyebrows. 'I *do* speak French, Ariana.'

'You have no right to address me by my first name.'

I knew Ariana well enough to know that she was hiding behind a fierce exterior and that she wanted exactly what I did at that moment – to shrink back in our seats until we became invisible.

The man's eyes glinted. 'Whether it be biological or not, I am still family. I believe this would make me your closest living relative, unless you count the other Moriarty brothers.'

'And where are they?' I found myself asking.

'One is a stationmaster in West England, and one is a colonel on his second term in India.'

There was a moment of silence during which Moriarty turned to survey the library's shelves. My sister broke it with what sounded like a warning.

'The town's not five miles away. I'm sure the police will be here soon since a telegraph would have been sent right away.'

Moriarty smiled with almost a hint of amusement in his eyes.

'Was that a threat or a warning? Logically, it can be neither. You cannot accuse me of killing your father.'

Suddenly emboldened, I retaliated. 'But we can prove that you stole that painting.'

'If I deny any involvement in the matter, Emily, with whom do you think the eyes of the law would find favour?'

My twin, her eyes blazing like a hateful predator, repeated her French contempt, along with several worse words of which I denied any understanding.

Moriarty did no more than draw a calm breath before speaking. 'And considering the circumstances, I think you'll find that it is inevitably unwise to turn me in.'

I glared at him with a fire worthy of the devil himself blazing in my eyes.

He began walking towards the door. 'Since I have nothing to do with the matter on a criminal basis, I really should find out what is going on.'

'Why are *you* inquiring, instead of the victim's own daughters?'

'For your own safety, I have told you to stay here, where you will not be exposed. You will be locked in until I return. There may still be a murderer in the house.' He turned, but stopped mid-step. 'Have you ever wondered why you were always kept so close to home?'

I swallowed hard and stayed still, thinking of my revelation concerning Earl Soham.

'Your father was always into something, incurring the wrath of certain people who have been seeking a way to silence him for years. It looks as if some of them have finally succeeded.'

As I stood at my bedroom's window, numbly wondering how real the last hour had been, I vaguely heard the door. Ariana's skirts rustled.

'The police ambulance is late. The officers are all waiting downstairs, taking the opportunity to speak to Mrs Thompson. They need nothing more from us besides the brief statements we already gave. We will have to speak at the inquest, but that won't be until next week.'

I turned away from the panes of glass, foggy with the air of a cool afternoon. 'Shall we proceed, then?'

My twin offered a half-hearted smile. 'Well, we certainly aren't going to get any information from the police.'

Hand in hand, we made our way to the first-floor hallway, past the ineffective attempts at a barricade, and into the study.

'When Moriarty came out, he asked Father to open the window. The door locked after. Did you overhear how Mrs Thompson discovered the body?'

'She was knocking to bring them another bottle of brandy. When there was no answer, she discovered that the door was locked, so she used her key.'

I closed my eyes, taking a steadying breath when my gaze instantly fell on the lifeless body of Sir Peter Ashford, formerly Moriarty, lying crumpled on the floor. The corpse was located close to halfway between the desk and the fireplace, with one arm stretched toward the carved furniture of polished cherry wood, felled right in front of the window behind the desk. A bullet hole gaped in the middle of his forehead, his face eternally frozen in shock.

'Did you hear if any weapon was to be found in the room?'

'No such thing turned up after a careful search.'

'And Mrs Thompson heard no gunshot?'

'Neither did we,' Ariana reminded me, 'and we were closer to the study than she was.'

A locked door. No weapon in the room. No sound of a gunshot. And yet there was a man dead with a bullet to the head.

Breathe deeply. If the room spins, make it stop.

I turned to the other indications of the room.

An empty bottle and two half-full glasses of amber-coloured brandy sat undisturbed on the desk. The window was open, a cool breeze filtering through. Nothing seemed out of the ordinary – besides the dead body, of course.

'The shooter must have fired through the window.' Wincing slightly, I stepped over my father to stand at the window. I put my hands on the sill to steady myself and leaned out, peering into the early dusk.

There was no way a shooter could have climbed through the window without scaling the brick outfacing like a tree frog. He also could not have gotten back down without landing in the flower beds. No one would be so unthinking. The roses were planted underneath the window, not in full bloom by any means, but a tangled mess of thorns nonetheless.

'Have we concluded that it was murder?' asked Ariana.

I turned my head to meet her gaze. 'Of course we have.'

Once back to the window, I mentally calculated the distance between it and the nearest tree: about one hundred yards. The next nearest possibility for a sniper's perch was the greenhouse roof: one hundred and fifty yards.

'You don't listen well, do you, Emily?' A voice came from the doorway, *not* my sister's.

My body stiffened.

The frighteningly familiar face of ex-professor James Moriarty was in the shadows of the threshold.

Ariana had turned to face him as well, seemingly as frozen as a block of ice.

'If you two will allow me to escort you back to your bedchamber to remain there until dinner, this shall stay between the three of us.'

Silently, we walked up the stairs, ducking behind a large tapestry for a moment when we heard some officers returning with the local coroner in tow.

'It's a baffling affair,' one officer said. 'Should we send for Scotland Yard? I've heard they have a private consultant whose success is unrivalled.'

An older, more experienced voice huffed. 'If we were going to send for the Mets, it should have been done earlier, lad. That time has passed.'

Their voices grew fainter. We continued on.

A few moments later, Moriarty let us into my bedroom and shut the door. I eyed my violin in the corner, wanting nothing more than to play through my entire music book to calm my not inconsiderably jangled nerves.

Ariana was shaking like a leaf. 'I found something earlier,' she whispered.

'What?'

She shook her head. 'Not now. He hears everything.'

Her words wrapped tight around my chest.

I walked to the window, for once not seeing beauty in the hills, but hiding spots for assassins; darkness rather than light.

I turned around, sinking to the floor, slumped against the wall. 'Father's dead for knowing what we do.'

I could see the same worry in Ariana's eyes.

We were next.

Chapter 6: To Guard the Guards

'But who is to guard the guards themselves?'
– Decimus Junius Juvenalis

I picked up my violin, holding up the bow to meet the instrument's strings. My eyes squeezed shut. I replaced the ornately carved, hollowed-out piece of wood back on a wicker chair, for my hands were shaking far too badly.

I sank down on my bed and held up a hand to massage my pulsing temple, gasping for breath as my throat closed tight. A single tear escaped me.

I realised how much I was letting myself slip. Part of it was the absence of my sister. She needed someone to hold her reins.

One tear. That was already more than I could afford now, and that was all I would cry for my father. There was nothing to mourn for, I had to convince myself of that.

I'd never really known him, nor had any real kinship with the man. Mother was the one who always sojourned with us, making sure we stayed close to home. Away from Earl Soham.

After her decline and eventual demise, Father restricted our movements even further. Visits to town were only to occur once a month under the strict supervision of one of the staff.

Not that the town had anything to offer us.

He never even enforced the rules himself – he left such things to the servants. He himself was always secluded, keeping to a tight schedule of breakfast, his office, luncheon, his office, dinner, his office, and bed.

By missing him, I would only be missing the sight of him at meals. *Nothing more.*

I sighed and stood up. Ariana had been gone far too long. It had been nearly two hours since she had confirmed that it was safe for her to go into the library as Moriarty was downstairs.

Father had always kept large volumes of ancestral records, including but not limited to the huge book I had consulted yesterday. We needed answers, and those volumes might hold some.

There were also financial records, I knew, which Father kept in the library rather than his study for "*security.*"

I absently picked at my nails. Why hadn't Ariana at least returned with the books so that we could investigate them together?

I quickly made my way to the door, opening it a crack to make sure the hallway was empty before slipping out. The path to the library was completely empty; I crept silently and undisturbed toward the huge double doors.

My heart pounded in anxiety. I wondered if they could hear it from downstairs.

The doors to the library creaked rather more loudly than I'd anticipated. I winced and, hands shaking, let them shut as slowly as possible.

'Ariana?' I whisper-called.

Merciful heavens, it was *exceedingly* cold here compared to the rest of the house.

And silent as a grave.

I paused when I heard the whistle of a summer breeze.

'Ariana?' I called again. My voice sounded weak and frightened, echoing all alone in the vast room.

There were no signs of anything – or anyone – unusual. I took a few hesitant steps toward the very back where I assumed my sister had set up a table filled with ancestral books to comb through. I kept calling her name in a soft, trembling voice, hoping for any answer at all.

As I passed through the bookshelves, I looked everywhere. Nothing seemed out of place. There wasn't a single particle of dust or a book removed from the shelves.

When we were younger, the room would echo with innocent laughter as we read through tales of trolls and dragons, ballads of knights and princesses, and stories of magic fairies and nymphs. We used to play hide-and-seek with Mother, squealing in mock fear when she found us.

Now the room was eerily silent, almost mocking the memories.

Reaching the back of the library, I stopped to scour the oval sitting area. There was no sign that anyone had been here, except that one of the windows was wide open. The curtains fluttered, dancing almost joyfully in the breeze.

After several moments of inspection, something stuck to a plush armchair jumped out at me. It was the same chair in which I'd been reading *Treasure Island* – could that only have been a few days ago?

It was a single hatpin, piercing a small piece of paper, torn hurriedly. I read it in haste:

Emily,

I know more than is safe. The numbers don't add up. It is not just him – he heads a criminal organisation. He is coming for me. And he will come for you too. Our half-brother, Dr. John Watson, lives at 221B Baker Street in London. You must flee there the moment you read this. Stop for nothing or no one. I hope to see you soon. Do not grieve if that is not to be.

Much love,
Ariana

Oh, no.

Please, no.

The window.

I ran, discarding the note and the hatpin.

Scuffs of shoe polish were visible right beneath the pane, as if there had been some sort of struggle. There was a small pooling of blood in the middle of which lay another of Ariana's hatpins. Specks of blood stained the curtains.

Had she used her pins in defence, or had they been taken and used against her? Was she injured? Was she even alive?

'My sister,' I murmured, feeling weak and fragile, as if I might crumple to the ground at any moment.

One thing was for certain: she was gone.

I was weak, alone, vulnerable. An easy target. It was only common sense that I would be eliminated next.

I had no choice but to flee.

Tonight.

I picked up the note Ariana had left. This was the last thing I had from her.

I made my exit quietly, letting the door slip shut behind me as I scouted the hallway. Still empty. As I took off quickly, carefully, up the stairs, all was silent. I did not hear a sound, even from downstairs.

Could it really be? I knew Ariana had enough common sense, but had no one heard her scream?

From beneath my bed, I pulled a cloth knapsack, much like something a reporter would carry. I had room for a few precious things.

I scouted the room, and carefully folded two extra dresses – one plain cotton and one with silk sleeves – and placed them in the bag. Next, I added Ariana's note and three small pictures, two of us together, one of them taken only a couple of months ago, and one of us with our mother. On top of that, I placed a brass magnifying glass which Mother had given us to study wildlife, and finally, fifty pounds in notes and coins.

My best walking shoes were already on my feet and I had slipped on extra petticoats under the dress I was wearing. I wore a dark blue velvet cloak with a pin of Ariana's and my sentimental golden locket around my neck. I slung the strap of the knapsack over my shoulder, blew out the single candle I had lit, slipping the room into darkness, and left as silently as I could.

Instead of taking the main way out, I hurried to the opposite end of the hallway, where I turned onto the servant's staircase, which led straight into the kitchen. I took a loaf of bread from the worn yet polished counter before quietly exiting through the back door.

The night was cool, but humid. Rain coming by midday tomorrow.

Crickets chirped in a calming chorus as I hurried to the stables.

With trembling hands, I saddled Catherine, my chestnut mare. I led her out of her stall, but the mare started prancing, feeling that something was off.

I stroked her side, quietly murmuring, 'It's all right, girl. There's nothing to worry about.'

Gradually she calmed down enough for me to lead her outside and jump on, kicking her into a steady run.

I knew the gates would be shut, especially tonight, so I turned Catherine gently towards the woods, and she followed my instructions dutifully. We crossed the border, riding swiftly into the forest. Tree branches and thorny bushes clawed at us, but as I steered my mount toward the old path, the obstacles disappeared, and Catherine's gait evened out.

After a stretch of time, Thorndon appeared in the form of some shadowy buildings ahead. I could not stay in town for the night. By morning – or perhaps before – someone at the Hall would find that I was missing and send word into town. The inn and hotel were undoubtedly closed and I'd have to catch the first train to London in the morning.

I knew from Father's schedule that the 7:15 train tomorrow was the first departure of the day headed to the Great Metropolis.

Near the edge of the forest, several weeping, overhanging trees created a shelter, and on the ground was a soft bed of moss. I stopped, realising that I had nothing to tie up Catherine with.

'Go home, girl,' I told her, knowing as I set her off in the direction of the estate that she could find her way. If not, then someone would find her quickly enough. Then, I removed the knapsack from my shoulder, setting it on the ground. I would spend the night here and catch the train in the morning. Resolved, I plopped down upon the ground, folding my legs under my dress comfortably.

As active as my brain was from recent events, I could not stay up all night. At some point, I began to shed unbidden tears for my beloved sister.

Eventually, I succumbed to sleep.

Chapter 7: One Braver Thing

> *'I have done one braver thing*
> *Than all the Worthies did;*
> *And yet a braver thence doth spring,*
> *Which is, to keep that hid.'*
> *– John Donne*

A shrill whistle hit a sour note close to my head. At first, I thought Ariana was attempting to wake me by playing my violin again.

'Put it down, sister,' I muttered, reaching sluggishly for the blankets. My hands found cloth, but it was strangely wet and not quilted at all. But, God have mercy, I was far too tired to worry about a bit of water on my bed.

The same shrill note sounded again, this time answered by a chorus of other noises of varying pitch.

Groaning, I forced my eyelids open. 'Ariana, you—'

I was not in my bed. Realisation hit that I was lying on top of a painfully hard tree root on the southeast edge of the forest, in sight of the town. The sky was dimly lit in the dingy grey of early morning. Mist swirled in abstract shapes, brushing the blades of dewy grass. A chorus of birds was singing gaily above my head.

The events of last night came flooding back, robbing my lungs of air and function. I shakily pushed myself up to a sitting position, wiping my hands on my magnificently grass-stained skirt.

I probably looked like I'd been through hell. Not that such a presumption would have been at all inaccurate.

I leaned my head back on the solid tree trunk behind me, watching as the green shapes rustled in the light breeze. My eyes slipped closed, a blissful memory from the past returning unbidden to the front of my mind.

Ariana poked her head down out of the tree, chestnut-brown locks falling into her face, and giggled.

'Em, come on!'

I sat up against a log, arranging acorns in neat rows. And for the multiplication problem of five times four, I would need five rows of four acorns each.

Sighing, Ariana dropped out of the tree and stood with her hands on her hips.

'Em!'

I looked dubiously over my shoulder at my exasperated sister. 'I don't think it's safe, Ariana.'

My twin untangled a twig from her hair and sighed once more. 'Em, you can't count on staying safe your whole life! We'll grow up, get married and move away from Mother and Father. And besides,' she shrugged. 'It's fun. We won't get hurt as long as we don't fall. And we won't get into any trouble as long as we don't rip our skirts.'

I stared into my sister's eyes, which pleaded for an adventurous companion, and stood up. 'All right.'

Resigned, I followed Ariana to the tree where she pulled herself up onto the lowest branch.

Climbing up to a higher branch, I giddily looked down at the world below and sighed contentedly. The risk was worth it to do what I wanted for once.

I opened my eyes again. My sister had been the one to convince me to give in to my adventurous nature that day. I hadn't regretted it since.

And now Ariana was gone.

I owed it to her to do everything in my power to ensure her safety and that monster's downfall.

Undoing my bag's strap, I noticed the loaf of bread on top and felt my stomach rumble. I broke off a small piece. My mouth was dry; I sorely wished I had some tea, or at least water. But hydration had not been a necessity when I left. I gingerly licked my lips and took another bite, trying not to appear too voracious even though my only company were the birds and chipmunks.

Having finished approximately half of the loaf, I returned it to my bag and made my way into town. Not many people were yet awake. Several young boys ran down the sidewalks, some with sticks, some with handfuls of stones. A man in a brown business suit sat on a bench by the train station reading a newspaper. As I stepped closer, I could plainly see the headline. My throat tightened.

Death of Sir Ashford Strikes Terror in Many

It was only natural that a sensational story such as this would be published within twenty hours of its occurrence. Particularly in such a small town. I didn't recognize the man and prayed he wouldn't recognize me either as I went to talk to him.

'Excuse me, sir, do you have the time?'

His eyes tore themselves reluctantly from the newspaper. His eyebrows raised as he looked me up and down, but he pulled a golden pocket watch from inside his coat and glanced at it. 'It's 6:43, miss.'

I thanked him with a nod and briskly walked away.

The hem of my dress caught my eye – it was snagged and torn and wet and smeared with dirt. I most likely looked the same all over. No wonder the man had given me such a once-over. He must have thought I'd wandered out of the forest after sleeping under a spell for twenty years, like *Rip Van Winkle* from the tale by Washington Irving.

God willing, I could find somewhere to clean up slightly. However, if it was nearly seven, I had no time. I had to make the 7:15 train and ensure Moriarty could not catch up with me. *But what were the chances that he hadn't caught on yet?*

Naturally, the despicable man would notice that I was missing soon, if he hadn't already. He would assume that I'd gone into town and that I would have bought a ticket to London on the closest train – where else would I go? Moriarty would come into town and ask if anyone had seen me, and the ticket-seller would tell him I'd bought a ticket on the 7:15 passenger express into London. The professor was a well-to-do man with much influential power; he would no doubt engage a private passenger train. Thus, he would reach London well before me, and be able to head me off.

My father being of the status he was, Thorndon had its own special, although I was sure it had never been used.

I could purchase a ticket for the first train, but I did not have to get on it. If only I could find some way to procure a ticket for the *next* express train to London without attracting attention…

But the first step was, of course, to get the decoy ticket.

I pushed as much hair as I could behind my ears – my hairpins had all fallen out – and approached the ticket-seller's booth.

'Miss Emily!' he exclaimed in surprise, looking up as I came nearer. His eyes widened, taking in my appearance. 'What happened to you?'

'I had a rough night,' I confessed. *Not a lie.* 'And walked into town this morning.' *Also not a lie.*

He nodded in understanding. 'And no wonder, with your father… I was sorry to hear, by the way.'

The man's expression had suddenly turned from shock to sympathy.

'Thank you for the condolences. I do, however, require a ticket for the 7:15 train.'

'London?' he said rather loudly. Then, looking uncomfortable, he lowered his voice. 'Why on earth do you need to go to London?'

'To see a relative.' *Not a lie.*

'Is Ariana not going?'

'No, I'm afraid she's needed at home.' *That* was a lie, and I felt strangely alright for telling it. But then the lack of guilt made me feel quite guilty indeed.

The ticket-seller's eyes betrayed his scepticism, but he silently handed me a ticket in exchange for some coins and wished me Godspeed on my journey.

Suddenly I heard a couple of the boys' voices calling out a greeting to someone entering town.

He was early.

I heard his voice over the rush of blood in my ears, asking the boys if they'd seen me. Hastily, I ducked into a side alley and crouched behind a box that smelt strongly of pigs, breathing hard. As if on cue, the final bell sounded from the platform – a small blessing. Escalating quickly in speed, the train pulled out of the station and was gone.

I faintly heard Moriarty begin a clipped interrogation. The ticket-seller immediately revealed that I'd bought a ticket on the 7:15 train to London, which had, unfortunately, just left.

Moriarty cursed angrily and began negotiating the price for a special.

I saw a young boy whose name was possibly Steven walk in front of my hiding spot and I saw my chance. Pulling him behind the crate, I put my index finger to his lips to silence him.

'What 'appened to yew?' the boy whispered.

'Very long story.' I handed him enough coins and instructed him to pay for a ticket for the next passenger express to London. 'Say your father asked you to buy it. Bring it straight back to me and don't say anything to that tall man over there and I can promise you a sovereign.'

The child's face brightened. He eagerly nodded and skipped off to fulfil the task he'd been given.

Not long after, I heard another train leaving the station at an even higher speed. Moriarty's special.

Even in the urgency of my situation, I felt my heart leap. It had worked. All I had left to do was make it onto the next train without the ticket-seller noticing.

The professor had fallen for my decoy. It would be hours before he realised the truth.

Steven returned, breaking me out of my thoughts. He handed over my ticket and I handed him the promised sovereign. The boy ran off, no doubt to spend his new treasure.

I glanced at the ticket: Passenger express to Paddington Station, 8:30 AM, 14th August, 1887.

I did not have a clue where that was located, nor did I have any idea how close it was to my destination. But I would figure it out when I got there.

If I was correct, I had just over an hour before my train left. Fortunately, this gave me time to freshen up.

As I headed towards the inn on the main road, I thanked the Almighty Lord that I'd thought to bring extra clothing.

One hour later, I stood on the platform of the Thorndon train station, wearing the silk and lace-lined gown I had carefully folded inside my satchel, with my hair pinned up under a wide-brimmed hat graciously given to me by the proprietor's wife.

I was by no means *clean*, for there had not been nearly enough time for that, but I was significantly neater in appearance. One might not have even linked me to the muddy, torn, bedraggled girl who had walked wearily into town earlier that morning.

The train whistle sounded sharply. The conductor gave the final warning for all passengers to board. Steam poured thickly into the air, dispensing rapidly as it fuelled my route to London.

By now, Moriarty would have realised that I had indeed not arrived in the Great Metropolis. He would have caught the train back to Thorndon to look for me. And by the time he returned, I would be a mere twenty-five miles from London.

I climbed aboard the train. It wasn't very crowded; there were only a scant few men in suits. Two of them appeared to be accompanied by women, their wives, most likely.

It wasn't at all hard to find a compartment for myself. As I locked the door and dropped my bag onto the seat, the train began to pull away from the platform, gathering speed with every second.

I sat down gingerly by the window and watched everything I'd ever known slip away, gulping down the fear of the approaching unknown.

Chapter 8: A Populous and Smoky City

> *'Hell is a city much like London –*
> *A populous and smoky city.'*
> *– Percy Shelley*

At approximately ten-thirty on the 14th of August, The Year of Our Lord 1887, my train pulled to a stop in Paddington Station.

London, at last.

My entire life I had dreamt of visiting our nation's great capital, full of well-dressed theatre-goers, men in tailored suits with cutaway trim and ladies bedecked in silk and jewels.

But judging by the sights and smells and sounds that greeted me, I couldn't have been more wrong. Before I even left my compartment, all my senses were assailed by the very essence of what London truly was.

The platform was utterly packed even though the day's travelling prime was hours away. There were people of all ages – from small, scrawny children to shabby and genteel men and women. I heard the incessant chatter of hundreds: boys selling newspapers, women calling for their children in proper and Cockney accents alike, screaming infants, and shouting men in the midst of a verbal donnybrook.

The air reeked of oil, dirt, foul smoke, and the stench of too many bodies packed too close together. Thankfully, it was the last of these senses to register.

Having spent so much time in the forest as a child, I was naturally accustomed to the dirt. The smoke was also a familiar beast, with the trains in town dispensing their used coal in the form of thick, black, rancid-smelling smoke.

Swinging the strap of my bag over my shoulder, I departed the train, taking a sweeping look at the many people crowding the platform. As soon as I stepped onto the platform itself, I felt the heavy throng immediately absorb me. Bodies bumped and jostled me. My forehead was soon damp from the heat of the crowd.

Finally at the entrance, I headed out as quickly as I could towards the street.

Outside, two men were leaning up against a low brick wall. One of them was tall, clean-shaven and dressed middle class – not shabby, nor especially well-to-do – while the other was shorter and scruffier in all respects, having the distinctive look of a sailor. Both were smoking inexpensive cigarettes.

The word *Thorndon* made me stop in my tracks.

'…haven't found out who did it,' said the tall man.

'Hmph. Never will, I reckon,' replied the short.

'They say Sir Ashford's business acquaintance was visiting the house at the time. Do you suppose he had anything to do with it?'

'Nah. They say he's a professor, as respectable as they come.'

Respectable.

I tasted bile, sour in the back of my mouth, and forced myself to swallow it.

With no desire to hear another word from them, I lifted my head, stood straight and stiff as a sophisticated lady, and walked in the direction of a cabstand about fifty yards away.

One of the cabbies loitering around was a portly man of average height. I needed a ride.

'You on yer own, miss?' he asked in a gravelly drawl.

'I am,' I replied cautiously.

Why did I say that? God forbid, what if he was out to kidnap a vulnerable girl and elicit her virtue out of her?

Instead, he continued to lean against the spindly fence, chewing his slimy tobacco lazily. 'Where to?'

'221B, Baker Street.' I had the address etched into my mind forever more, as I had hardly done anything but stare at the note for most of the two-hour train ride.

'That'll be three shillings.'

I carefully counted out the money from the small pouch inside my satchel and dropped it into the man's calloused hand. He pocketed the coins casually and held open the door of the cab.

Inside was a single bench made to seat a maximum of two, and a sliding window with a clear view of the front. The back had a seat for the driver, onto which he promptly climbed. While I was unfamiliar with the capital, I knew of its famous hansom cabs.

As we started moving, I tried to pay attention to the streets we passed, where we turned, and the speed we were moving. The wheels rolling over cobblestone made the cab rock back and forth unsteadily. We couldn't go overly fast, due to other cabs and people crowding the streets.

A group of children chased each other merrily, not heeding the large carriages and horses that could easily crush them without stopping.

I was so concentrated on my surroundings that I barely noticed the time. It seemed not even fifteen minutes had passed until we reached Baker Street. Before I had time to prepare myself for it, the cab pulled to a halt. I stepped out cautiously, careful to avoid the muck on the street. Behind me, the cab rattled off, dissolving into the chaos of London, and I was left standing on the sidewalk alone.

The building in front of me was nondescript, made of worn and fading brick. It appeared to be part of a series of row-houses, with a brass number affixed beside the door that read *221B*.

It seemed just like any other common building I'd seen in London so far. Did my half-brother truly live *here*?

Growing up, I'd always thought if I had a relative living in London, they would own a fashionable, elaborate manor house by the river. But if my first impressions of Paddington Station were a good basis, London was not at all what I'd envisioned. Now I had no idea what I should expect. Perhaps this was as fancy as the Great Metropolis got.

Now that I had finally reached my destination, fears began to surface once again in my mind. What if no one would help me? What if I had the wrong address? What if Ariana's information was wrong and I didn't have a half-brother at all? A million questions swirled in my mind, filling me with doubt and nausea.

Ignoring my unease, I stepped forward and rang the bell.

Not a moment later the door was answered by a woman who looked to be in her mid-forties. She wore a plain, flowered frock with a flour-covered apron overtop. She looked me up and down, her eyes soft and gentle.

'May I help you?' she asked, a faint trace of a Scottish lilt in her voice.

'Yes, I'm looking for Doctor Watson,' I said, hoping against hope that my voice wasn't as timid and squeaky as it sounded.

'Of course, dear.'

The woman opened the door wider and allowed me to step inside. I found myself standing in a simple yet elegant foyer. An oriental carpet covered the wooden floorboards, and vases of flowers adorned the banister of the stairs. A coat rack and an umbrella stand stood near the door. I could not help noticing that among the umbrellas and walking sticks were an army officer's ceremonial sword and a harpoon. My brow furrowed.

What an eccentric collection of belongings.

'Do you have a card, dear?' asked the woman in a hospitable voice, pausing at the foot of the stairs.

'Er – no,' I replied foolishly. Of course, a lady of my standing should always carry visiting cards. However, I had never had any need for them as I had never been visiting.

'That's all right,' she assured, and gestured for me to follow her up the stairs.

Wanting to remember everything about this experience, I sternly commanded myself to notice all the details I could. As we ascended the stairs, I counted seventeen.

At the landing, the woman stopped and knocked lightly on a door.

'Yes, come in!' called an aristocratic voice from within.

She turned the knob and poked her head around the door. 'There is a young lady here for Doctor Watson.'

Suddenly pushed forward, I entered the room in a state; my mouth dropped open in shock at what I saw.

The room was lined with red-patterned wallpaper. On one wall, there was a series of small round holes – almost like bullets – that formed the letters *VR*. A desk stood to the left of the door, cluttered with stacks of files and paperweights and knickknacks in general. A second desk stood to the right, much more neat and orderly. On the opposite side of the room were bookshelves crammed with what appeared to be scientific essays, encyclopaedias, and various other literary accomplishments. In the far-right corner, there was a stained old table covered with many different tubes, vials, and containers of liquid and powder in various shades.

The sitting area consisted of a sofa and two armchairs, angled to face the fireplace directly across the room. Closer to the fireplace, there was a wicker chair with two cushions for comfort.

Objects on the mantelpiece included a single red rose, a jack-knife skewering a pile of papers to the surface on which they lay, a single scuffed and worn Persian slipper, and what appeared to be a human skull.

But most shocking of all was that there were two men in the room, both perfectly at home. One was a tall, thin, pale-skinned man with long, spidery fingers and dark brown hair. He stood near the window by the stained table. Meanwhile, the other man was slightly shorter, portlier, and sporting a moustache. His hair was a lighter shade of brown, more chestnut. His deep, hazel-brown eyes betrayed kindness and compassion. I knew that if I looked into a mirror, I would find the very same ones staring back at me.

There was no doubt that this was the man for whom I had come.

'I don't remember you making an appointment today, Watson,' said the tall man, sounding quite interested.

'Neither do I, Holmes,' said my brother.

Why did that name sound so familiar?

'Are you Doctor Watson?' I asked, nodding in the direction of the man with the moustache.

'I am. And this is my dear friend and colleague, Mr Sherlock Holmes.'

And suddenly I knew where I had heard the name before – on a stone walkway, beside my twin sister, staring at the face of the man I now knew had killed my mother.

'There is a man whose success I have been following for some time. He has much more talent than any of the professionals, yet he calls himself an amateur… When the police find themselves with a case beyond their limits, they bring it to Sherlock Holmes, the remarkable reasoner, who can often bring cases to a close without ever leaving the comfort of his sitting room.'

My half-brother lodged with the man whose attention Moriarty desperately sought.

'And you are?' asked Doctor Watson politely.

'Emily,' I answered shakily. 'Miss Emily Watson.'

'A Watson.' Sherlock Holmes raised his eyebrows. 'What a remarkable coincidence, eh, Doctor?'

'Quite so. Miss Watson, may I inquire what I can help you with?'

So, it really wasn't obvious to him.

'You mean that you didn't know?'

His brow furrowed in confusion.

'Doctor Watson, I'm your half-sister.'

Chapter 9: No Longer Peace

'If peace cannot be maintained with honour, it is no longer peace.'
– Lord John Russell

'I'm sorry, my *what?*'

It was almost a full minute before he replied, looking very much like he was choking on a particularly large oyster.

'For the sake of practicality I will assume that you heard me.'

I noticed that Mr Holmes' mouth was agape, and it was to him that I turned. 'I was hoping that you could help me.'

The two men snapped their mouths closed.

'Pray tell us, Miss Watson, what is wrong?' asked the amateur detective.

Drawing a breath, I found that I was gaining confidence in speaking, my fears shrinking by the minute.

'Perhaps you have read in the newspapers of the murder of Sir Peter Ashford.'

Both men's faces immediately showed recognition. After exchanging a glance, they nodded slowly.

'He was my stepfather.'

The doctor drew a sharp breath. 'I am terribly sorry for your loss, Miss Watson—'

'Emily,' I interjected. 'We *are* family.'

'Begging your pardon, Miss Watson, but we have just been introduced. Now, am I to understand that your father was…'

'The same as yours? Yes. After your mother died, he remarried my mother, Leanne. I assume you and your father have not spoken in quite some time.'

Doctor Watson looked uncomfortable. 'He died when I was in the army, but we had not spoken for some years prior.'

I nodded and continued my story. 'Together they had two children, twins, myself and—'

'Ariana,' Holmes finished for me. He had no doubt already read the newspapers.

I affirmed it, then settled my gaze back on my brother. 'When our father died, my mother remarried. My sister and I were barely a year old.'

Doctor Watson murmured his sympathy, but Holmes looked impatient.

'Would you mind terribly, Miss Watson, if we returned to the reason you have come here?'

'Not at all. Two days ago my stepfather was visited by a man he introduced to us as his business acquaintance. Ariana and I found it an obvious lie. The man was invited by my father to stay at the house for a few days.

'Through the course of some investigating, my sister and I discovered that the man was my stepfather's brother. His motives for visiting and my father's motives for lying about it are unclear.'

Oh, I cursed how easy the lie was coming now!

'Yesterday afternoon I overheard them speaking in my father's study, where our guest was accused of having my mother killed. He did nothing to deny it. But he seemed to know of my eavesdropping and he confronted my sister and I in the library. That's when the call of murder rang out. And you, gentlemen, know the rest.'

My brother appeared ready to soothe me, but Holmes merely gazed sharply through keen eyes of steel.

'You are travelling alone,' he said, cocking his head.

'Yes, and you have obviously deduced that from the fact that I have my bag with me. If I were with a companion, they would either be here with me, or else I would not have my belongings on me. If I were only dropped off here, then my companion would be headed to our hotel, where they would no doubt have taken my baggage to be deposited in my room. Thus, I am here alone and with no place to stay.'

Both men appeared astonished that I caught on to Holmes' parlour tricks so easily. However, the detective quickly recovered.

'Yes, but I would like to know *why* you are alone, and what could have caused your trip to be so abrupt. Where is your sister?'

'My sister is gone.'

Holmes leapt to his feet and began to pace with all the energy of a foxhound on the trail. 'Gone? What do you mean by *gone?*'

'She found out too much,' I forced myself to say. 'Someone kidnapped her late last night. She left me a note with this address, telling me to flee from the house immediately.'

'Do you have the note?'

'No, but I can quote it to you.'

Why was I lying? Did I really not yet trust these men? It was merely an instinctual feeling. If my brother was as emotional as Ariana and I, he would be bound to react rashly.

And so I recited the note, only leaving out the bit about Moriarty heading a criminal organisation. While I spoke, Holmes sat down in an armchair, leaning forward intensely.

'Who is this *he,* this guest of your father's you keep mentioning?'

'We do not know his name,' I said quickly, with a glance at my newfound half-brother. I did not want him involved with the matter. Particularly if Moriarty could make people disappear as swiftly as he had stolen Ariana. I would only drag him into this if it became absolutely necessary.

Holmes looked as if he would love nothing more than to argue that he could not make progress on the case without a name. Thankfully, he did not.

Not a second later I cocked my head, listening to a barely audible commotion from the foyer. 'There is a very distressed young boy downstairs.'

'However could you—' began my brother.

Holmes looked surprised as well.

'My dear doctor, I have done more than my fair share of eavesdropping.'

Only a minute passed before the sitting room door burst open, revealing a small, scrawny lad, not more than 10 years of age, pink-faced and out of breath.

'Peter!' exclaimed Holmes. 'What's the matter, my fellow?'

'Wig's sick,' the boy rasped between gasps for air. 'Oi figgered oi should come fer yew, Doctor Watson.'

I hadn't a clue what connection this child – who clearly lived on the streets – had to Holmes and my brother, nor did I know who "Wig" was, but it seemed to spring the doctor into immediate action.

That was when Peter noticed me, and his cheeks went pinker still. 'Oi'm sorry, Mr 'Olmes, oi didn't know yew 'ad company.'

'Never you mind that, Pete, how is he sick?' asked my brother, reaching for his medical bag behind the table.

'Well, 'e's real 'ot, and 'e tosses and turns. Been sleepin' since last night.'

I couldn't be sure, but I thought I heard Doctor Watson curse under his breath as he followed the child out the door.

Holmes must have observed my questioning glance, for he quickly explained. 'Peter is one of my Baker Street Irregulars. They are a group of young boys – orphans, mostly – who serve as the unofficial force. They are my eyes and ears on the street. Wiggins, the leader, has evidently taken ill.'

'How long will he be gone?'

Holmes shrugged lightly, fingers tapping on the arm of his chair and staring out the window absently. 'It depends. Most likely an hour or more. Odd timing.'

It was indeed. I found myself wondering idly about the reaches of an alleged criminal organisation. However suspiciously convenient, this gave me time to explain my true situation to Holmes. I had no idea I would be seeing him, but as long as I was, there could be no harm in enlisting his help.

'Perfect,' I said quietly. 'Then, allow me to fill in the blanks I left in my story.'

'It was peculiar that your stepfather would not have introduced his visitor, nor had Ariana uncovered his name during her research.'

'I am sorry I could not speak freely in front of Doctor Watson. It is a matter of family, and I don't want him personally involved.'

'But is Doctor Watson not family?'

'Yes, he is a Watson. Which, correct me if I'm wrong, means that he worries far too much.'

Something like amusement crossed Holmes' face; he quickly looked away.

I wrapped my arms around myself and worried my fingers against the seam of my bodice.

'There is also danger. My sister is already gone. I will not risk the brother I have just found as well.'

'I understand, Miss Watson. Would you be kind enough to tell me who this guest of your stepfather was?'

'Did you read in the papers Wednesday last of the painting stolen from the Museum at the University of St. Andrews?'

He looked surprised. 'Why, yes I did. A singular affair. The papers neglected to name the man they suspected.'

'They were likely paid to keep it quiet. It was a professor, who was thus removed from his post.'

Holmes eyed me quizzically. 'Why would you say they were paid off?'

'I'll get to that.'

'This is turning out to be a very twisted web.'

'Yes. The man who stole the painting is my stepfather's brother. He came to my father to ask for help.'

'What sort of help? Was your stepfather an influential man?'

'I don't know.'

'What, then, was this Professor Ashford's motive for stealing the painting?'

'Not Ashford.'

'But they are brothers, no?'

'Ashford was not my father's true surname.' My voice was beginning to tremble. 'He changed it to avoid connection with his family.'

Holmes looked at me expectantly, as if he were barely restraining himself from drawing out every detail from me forcibly. I took a breath to calm my nerves, which were ignited by the fire of rage in my heart whenever I thought of the man.

'The professor who stole the painting – that is to say my stepfather's brother – goes by the name of James Moriarty.'

Holmes' eyebrows lifted.

'It appears that you have heard the name?'

The detective nodded. 'He's a scientific genius. He's written nearly two dozen mathematical theorems and essays, all of which are baffling to the average mind. Are you suggesting that he is responsible for—'

'I did not quote to you the entire note, Mr Holmes. And I do have it with me.'

I quickly moved to open my satchel, still by my side, and pulled out the torn piece of paper filled with my sister's rushed penmanship. Holmes took it from my grasp, scanning it over in five seconds.

'An organisation?'

I nodded. 'I have no doubt that he gave the order for my father to be killed. He had the window opened so the origin of the bullet could not be traced.'

'You seem quite confident of this fact. Can you tell me what exactly it was you heard them speaking of in your stepfather's study?'

'I suppose.' I thought back to the conversation. *Had it only been yesterday?* I explained to him about my father's name change and Moriarty speaking about his "chance for redemption".

'And the conversation you overheard in the study?'

'The first thing I heard was Moriarty telling my father that he would regret something. I can only assume this was his refusal to help his brother out of a tight spot. The conversation progressed to my father directly accusing him of having my mother killed. As I previously stated, Moriarty did nothing to deny the fact.'

'But did he confirm it?'

I mentally ran over the conversation, and repeated the most suspicious part of the conversation as I heard it in my head.

'Why did you kill her?'

'She may have threatened me, Peter, but I am certainly not responsible for her death...'

Once I was done, Holmes thought for a long moment.

'Did you ever find his motives for stealing the painting?'

'No.' A lie. 'But we did find a paper while searching my father's study two nights ago that confirmed he was the mathematics professor at the University of St. Andrews. There is no doubt that it was him.'

The detective was silent and I feared he was sceptical.

'You do agree with me, don't you, Mr Holmes?'

'He is playing a game of his own design… I have long been aware of some distinguished malefactor in the higher criminal world. Some large organisation with many agents well hidden in various places.'

I had been staring at my lap. Now I snapped my head up to stare at him. 'Do you think this is it?'

'I cannot yet be sure.'

I leapt up from my seat and began to pace the hearthrug.

'I hardly knew my stepfather, so that wasn't the hardest of blows. Rest assured, I've endured harder. But we – *I* – cannot allow him to get away with taking my sister. He's wronged me once, twice, now three times. He's taken from me the three people I love most. I'm sure you understand, Mr Holmes, that I *need* your help.'

'You *need* closure. Who's to say I can give you that?'

I considered, not for the first time, telling him of Moriarty's interest in his career, but – perhaps selfishly – decided against it. Moriarty wanted Holmes' attention, but I could not give that bastard what he wanted. He owed me and I would yield nothing to him in fighting for my sister. This wasn't about Holmes; his being here was sheer coincidence.

Or was this all by Moriarty's design?

I bottled the war inside my chest.

'I could go to Scotland Yard, if you like. But trust me, Mr Holmes, this is not something you want to miss being a part of. '

'No. It is likely with them that you wouldn't succeed.'

As he spoke this piece of advice, I noted that his voice dripped with disdain.

'So you think it is worth investigating?'

'I most definitely think it is worth looking into.'

I took a deep breath. 'Moriarty has now killed both my parents, and taken my sister, but I fear we haven't much to go on.'

Chapter 10: Profound Secret and Mystery

'A wonderful fact to reflect upon, that every human creature is constituted to be that profound secret and mystery to every other.'
– Charles Dickens

'What exactly is it that we know?' Holmes asked me, his voice level.

My stomach churned. I still couldn't tell him the truth. If I did, he'd know I'd lied to him. He might refuse me his help. Then what would I do? I'd dug myself into a hole that I was too ashamed to climb out of.

'He taught at the University of St. Andrews, stole that painting, was discreetly removed from his post to avoid scandal, and came to Thorndon to ask his biological brother for help. When my father refused, he had him killed. The man runs a criminal organisation – a fact my sister found out about, causing her abduction,' I said, leaving out the bit about Holmes once again.

'How did you and your sister come to know he stole the painting?'

I explained about our search of Father's study and the connection we made, having observed the pamphlet in his coat pocket from the unveiling of the Vernet canvas.

'And yet you could not, despite your best efforts, discover what he wanted with the painting?'

'We confronted him about it in the northwestern passageway. He merely threatened us.'

'How?'

'He told us we were meddling in affairs that were not our business, and that curiosity always kills the cat.'

'And that was all?'

'That was all.' I should've felt remorse in telling the lie, but did not.

'Is there anything else I should know about this Moriarty or your stepfather's relation to him?'

'There was something about the family casting off my father because he wasn't like the rest of them, and then he changed his name to avoid being associated with them.'

'And do you know if he ever was associated with his family?'

'I can only assume he was, at some point. The Moriarty estate is only twenty miles from Thorndon. Even though he was intensely antisocial, my father was well-liked enough in town, and if they knew anything about his heritage, they didn't let it on.'

'Did you ever visit the vicinity of the Moriarty estate?'

'No, we were not allowed more than twenty miles from home, likely to avoid our visiting the estate, but our boundaries meant we never had reason to go beyond the limits of Thorndon.'

'But he never actually told you this?'

'No, it was merely a theory I had – and, to my knowledge, a very likely one.'

'So you have nothing concretely explaining it?'

Like a firecracker exploding into the sky, Moriarty's words popped into my head:

'Your father was always into something, incurring the wrath of certain people who have been seeking a way to silence him for years. It looks as if some of them have finally succeeded.'

'He said this before leaving the room to "investigate" the cry of murder,' I told Holmes.

'You said your stepfather rarely left the grounds, correct?'

'Hardly ever, to my memory. But his schedule was so reclusive that I only saw him during select parts of the day. He could have done anything while under the premise of working in his office.'

'Have you any vague idea who these certain people may be?' Holmes asked eagerly. 'Anyone with whom your father had any altercations?'

I shrugged. 'As I said, he hardly left the house at all. He always kept to himself; he drove himself into further seclusion after my mother passed. It was a miracle if he ever spoke to anyone, let alone enough to have an argument. The only exception being Moriarty, his own brother, whom I suspect my father hadn't seen since he left them.'

'And you have absolutely no clue who killed him?'

'No more than you do, Mr Holmes. You know from the newspapers that the window was opened, and the shot likely came from one hundred to one hundred and fifty yards away. My father was shot directly in the head and most likely died a quick death.'

Still, I paced the length of the hearthrug. I knew if I sat down again, my legs would be shaking from sheer restlessness.

Holmes lapsed into silence, his head resting on one hand, staring moodily into space. Then, he abruptly stood up and pulled a rope beside the dinner table, ringing a bell somewhere else in the house.

A moment later the woman from earlier reappeared.

'Ah, Mrs Hudson, would you bring up luncheon for three? Doctor Watson can eat when he returns.'

'Yes, Mr Holmes,' said Mrs Hudson, and began to turn away.

'Oh, and Mrs Hudson?'

'Yes, dear?'

'Kindly step outside and ask the constable in front of the door to go fetch Inspector Lestrade.'

She nodded and walked away briskly.

'Is she the housekeeper?' I asked, thinking of Mrs Thompson back home.

'Actually, she's our landlady.'

'And who, pray tell, is Inspector Lestrade?'

'He is from Scotland Yard.'

I raised an eyebrow. 'I thought they wouldn't be of much help.'

'They can be of assistance on occasion, especially in gathering information on larger cases.'

'I see.' I picked at a loose thread on my sleeve anxiously. I spoke up again in a moment, drawing Holmes' attention. 'I had no clue until today that you lived here. I was only informed of this address as that of my half-brother, Doctor Watson.'

'You've heard of me, though?'

Once again I remembered Moriarty's words and felt myself sicken.

'You could say that.'

The sound of footsteps upon the stair echoed in the room just then, and Holmes courteously opened the door for Mrs Hudson, bearing a heavily laden tray.

All traces of nausea vanished at the sight. I realised that all I'd eaten today was the bit of bread this morning, with a cup of tea on the train.

Holmes pulled out a chair for me with a nod. I gave him a grateful smile, sitting down. He took the seat across from me.

I placed two sandwiches onto my plate. They appeared to be made with ham, cheese, and lettuce. As I took a bite, my stomach rumbled appreciatively. My hunger was still not satisfied after consuming them in less bites than was ladylike, but did not think it would seem very polite to go for seconds, so I merely sat, sipping my tea.

Holmes studied me covertly for a moment (though I did indeed know he was watching), then picked up the tray. 'We wouldn't want you to remain so hungry. Please, take more.'

I smiled at him and obliged, taking another sandwich. Another minute had passed before I realised that the detective was still staring at me.

'Yes?' I prompted, setting down my teacup.

'Is there anything... else I should know about you?'

'Pardon?'

'You no doubt have an excellent eye for details. And I can see that you play the violin, and are no doubt accustomed to horseback riding and other... rigorous activities.'

How much was safe to say? How much could he handle?

'Well,' I began, carefully choosing my words, 'I was schooled by my mother, before her death, in the sophisticated arts of the gentry – embroidery and stitching, dancing and etiquette – though by no means did I enjoy them. Nor have I ever had much occasion to employ them. I am rather an adventurous sort; I would venture to say that my potential has been wasted in my years under tight reins. I will read anything under the sun and write if I had anything to write about. I sketch and paint, but only landscapes – and not well, may I add. I also speak a few languages.'

Adding anything else would be a stretch.

It was then that I heard footsteps on the stairs. I cocked my head as the detective opened his mouth to reply. 'Would that be…'

Holmes went to open the door. 'Hello, old chap.'

Inspector Lestrade of Scotland Yard turned out to be a short, quite thin man; his eyes looked tired and his chin was covered in stubble.

'Haven't been home in two days, I see. The Fulson case?'

'Yes, indeed, Holmes.' Lestrade sounded weary but alert. 'And who is the guest?'

'Ah. She is the reason I called you here.'

'Is she a client?'

'In a manner of speaking, yes.'

Holmes nodded in my direction. I stood up and extended my hand for a shake.

'Emily Madeline Watson, sir. A pleasure.'

The Scotland Yard officer took my hand, and I blushed when he kissed it. It was a sign of respect, I knew, but I had been aiming for professionalism and maturity. Then, it was as if my name caught up to him in slow motion. His eyebrows shot up.

'As in *Doctor* Watson?'

'Yes, I am his half-sister, sir.'

'Miss Watson has discovered that her stepfather's brother, Professor James Moriarty, runs a large criminal organisation. He has orchestrated the deaths of her mother and stepfather and, as far as we know, has abducted her sister, Ariana.'

'Would this be in connection with the death of Sir Peter Ashford?'

'He was my stepfather, sir.'

'My condolences,' Lestrade offered a slight nod.

'I thought we should involve the official force in a case of this magnitude.' Holmes' face was very serious. 'We haven't very much information to go on, I'm sorry to say.'

'And why isn't Doctor Watson here?'

The amateur detective exchanged a glance with me before replying. 'He's with a patient, but we thought it best for him not to know.'

'So we're proceeding without his knowledge, then?' Lestrade's eyes suddenly assumed a professional glint.

'Yes, we are.'

The officer took a seat on the wicker chair by the unlit fireplace. 'Very well. What is known?'

Chapter 11: Cunning Sin

> *'O! What authority and show of truth*
> *Can cunning sin cover itself withal.'*
> *– William Shakespeare*

Inspector Lestrade slowly shook his head.

'An organisation of crime. Holmes, you know I'll have to run this by the Commissioner's Office.'

'No.' Holmes' voice was sharp as a sabre.

'It's a complete breach of protocol!'

'Don't you think it likely that Moriarty has agents planted in numerous places, including the police force?'

'Surely you don't think—'

'My dear inspector, how else do you imagine he has been able to pull off a scheme of this magnitude? He seems to be toying with the authorities at every turn.'

Sherlock Holmes made an excellent point, and I could tell that Lestrade knew it too by the way his Adam's apple bobbed.

'Very well. However, if I am caught withholding information, I will implicate you, Holmes.'

'Understood, inspector.'

'I should hope so. Now, there are a few details of another case I need to make sure the Home Office is informed of. With your consent, I shall take my leave.'

'Thank you, Lestrade.'

'A good day to you, inspector,' I said, smiling politely.

As the door shut with a soft click, I turned to stare at Holmes.

'Do you distrust the Commissioner's Office that much?'

'I will say that Commissioner Lynch is far less inept than Harrison was, but he still isn't the most competent of fellows in the string of them the Yard has recently seen.'

'But how do you expect to progress without the full support of the Force behind us?'

'It will take time,' said Holmes slowly, no doubt pondering his choice of words, 'and it will be a tough journey, but with a measure of strength and perseverance, we will make sure that light is shined upon this gruesome matter.'

'How long before we know enough to alert the public?'

'I can tell you that it won't be any time soon. It will require quite a bit of surreptitious sleuthing on my part.'

'Why not on mine? If anything, I'm even more a part of this than you are!'

'Moriarty *knows* you, Emily,' the detective said apologetically. His use of my first name took me aback.

He knows you too, I thought bitterly. But would it dissuade him from personally attempting to infiltrate Moriarty's syndicate or fuel the spark that I could see in his eyes?

I stared at the oriental carpet on the floor and stayed silent.

'Until we can plot a safe and thorough course of action, however,' Holmes brought me back to the present, 'I suggest we wait for the good doctor to return.'

Days passed like sand slipping into the bottom of an hourglass. Over the next week, I found myself observing the two men with interest, even growing used to the living habits of my half-brother and the rather eccentric Sherlock Holmes. They seemed to be the closest of friends, talking, laughing and smiling at each other as though gazing upon a work of art. Once, I even observed the detective tousle the doctor's hair fondly, at which the latter smirked and flicked up his friend's collar as he tried to duck away.

It was upon the afternoon of the 21st of August that I found myself alone in the flat. Even Mrs Hudson had gone to the flower stands of Covent Garden – a place I had learnt was quite popular.

I was pacing the hardwood floor of my new bedroom. It was a cheerily decorated spare room at the top of the seventeen stairs that the landlady had kindly prepared for me. Here is where I allowed my mind and imagination to wander, in lieu of the answers I wanted so desperately.

Holmes had hardly been present at 221B Baker Street since my arrival. I hadn't a clue what he was working on or if he'd discovered anything pertaining to the Moriarty case. If he had come up with new leads, I would have liked to be informed. And if he was on a different case entirely, I would have relished the opportunity to give my idle brain a challenge of any sort. How could I find out without asking him directly?

He kept all records and correspondence pertaining to his current cases on his desk, as far as I knew. And snooping did happen to be what I did best.

Slipping into my shoes so as not to trod in only my stockings, I turned the doorknob and stepped out of my room. As soon as I set foot in the hallway, I could sense some presence in the house. Silently, I crept in the direction of the sitting room.

The door was already slightly ajar. I pushed it open to survey the scene and froze. There was a man sitting casually on the sofa with his legs crossed, smoking, as if this were his home.

'Hello, Miss Watson,' said Professor Moriarty.

Cautiously, I entered the room, but stayed near the door.

'What the blazes are you doing here?'

He chuckled. 'Mind your language, Miss Watson. You thought I didn't know this was where you'd gone?'

Were there any possible weapons I could reach in time?

'I admit you had me at first,' he continued. 'Buying that decoy train ticket was a very nice touch. I had no idea what you'd done until I reached London. Then, of course, I had to return to Thorndon and test the ticket-seller's memory a little bit further.'

I swallowed.

Moriarty raised one eyebrow. 'How much does Holmes know?'

'What are you talking about?' My voice shook.

You know exactly what he's talking about.

'Did you tell him about his great-great-great-uncle's painting?'

'Yes.'

'So he knows why it was stolen, correct?'

My mouth didn't seem to remember how to work.

'No,' I finally admitted.

'I thought not.' Moriarty's mouth twisted into a wry smile.

'You never answered my question. Why are you here?'

'It is to warn you, Miss Watson.' He was grinding out his cigarette in an ashtray sitting among scattered papers on the side table. Grimacing, he held up the butt. 'Your brother's. Not my usual. But it would pain me to have to act against your curiosities. I do not wish to reunite you and your sister in that way.'

My heart struggled against my ribcage, loud in its resistance.

'What have you done with her?' I asked in a low voice, still barely controlling my rage.

He chuckled, a deep, menacing sound I had hoped to never hear again. 'Do not worry yourself, Miss Watson, your sister is still alive. She is in a safe place, far from causing any more trouble.'

'You will pay for this.'

Moriarty picked up his hat and cane from where they rested beside the door. 'Fortunately, my dear, I have money to spare.'

I stared after him with venomous eyes as he descended the stairs with surprising agility.

'Good day, Miss Watson,' he called almost jovially as he opened the door. It shut just as quickly behind him.

Crossing to the window, I pushed aside the curtain and watched my tormentor step into a waiting carriage. Watching him slip away once again caused a lump to form in the back of my throat. With a silent curse, I sank shakily onto the floor.

I had hardly shed a tear since coming to Baker Street – in fact, I had not cried since the night I escaped Thorndon Hall. But not knowing what else to do, I began to sob.

Mrs Hudson returned sometime later and I retired to my bedroom before she could inquire of my state. I claimed a slight headache, but no, she should not send for my brother to return from his club.

On the way out I took the cigarette Moriarty had smoked from the ashtray and threw it out my window.

Collapsing onto my bed, my tears renewed. I felt vulnerable, helpless. There didn't seem to be anything I could do but cry.

This is completely pointless, I decided a few hours later, as I sat on my bed. *Holes don't undig themselves – especially not ones that grow more dangerous the deeper they become.*

It might be too late to completely mend the mistake, but it would do no good to keep it a secret forever. It would certainly be worse if he were to discover the truth on his own. And since Moriarty could evidently get into the house without any problems, I couldn't go on putting others at risk.

Holmes needed to know the whole truth.

Wiping the traces of tears from my eyes, I silently made my way to the sitting room. I entered to find John seated on the sofa, in the same seat Moriarty had occupied just hours before.

'Is Holmes here?'

'I am afraid he is not.' John put down his newspaper to study my face with a physician's critical eye. 'Are you quite all right, my dear? You've missed dinner entirely, and you look rather pale.'

I shook my head. 'I'm fine, thank you. There was merely something I wished to discuss with Holmes. Do you have any idea where he's gone, or when he'll be back?'

'I don't. May I help you?'

'No, thank you. Please don't bother yourself over me.'

And without further explanation or words of any kind, I turned and left the room, descending the stairs with every intention to wait for Holmes in the foyer – all night if necessary.

At the bottom of the steps, I very nearly collided with the landlady who was carrying a stack of freshly pressed linens.

'Mrs Hudson,' I reached out to stop her. 'Did Holmes happen to tell you anything about where he was going, or when he'd be back?'

She smiled apologetically. 'Not a thing, dear. He was just up and out the door, off on some foxhunt of his, I'm sure.'

'Thank you.'

Sitting down in the upholstered chair by the coat rack, I curled my legs up under my skirt, settled into a semi-comfortable position and began to wait. My eyes began to droop as the grandfather clock counted the minutes. *Tick, tick, tick.*

I awoke to a gentle hand shaking my shoulder. When I opened my eyes, I was startled to find Holmes bent over me, his Inverness cloak soaking wet.

'What on earth happened to you?'

'I took an unexpected dip in the Thames,' the detective flippantly waved his hand. 'What you must speak to me about has to be urgent, if you would wish to accost me almost as soon as I walked in the door.' He knelt. 'Pray tell me, what is the matter?'

'It's to do with Moriarty. And the painting. And you.'

Holmes' eyebrows raised but his perfectly controlled attitude showed no other signs of surprise. His face remained otherwise passive, gazing intently at me with sharp eyes that were the colour of steel.

'With me?'

I took a deep breath. 'Moriarty came to visit this afternoon.'

'*Here?*'

I nodded, my gaze fixed on the ground. 'He said he came to warn me to stay off the case, that he does not wish to do to me as he did to Ariana.'

'And did he say what that was?'

'He said he did not kill her, but that she was in a safe place where she would not cause trouble.'

'Emily, why did you not send a message to Scotland Yard immediately?'

I averted my gaze for a long moment before looking up to meet his gaze. 'Because there was something I needed to tell you and you alone.'

He cocked his head at me before replying. 'Come up to the sitting room. I'm sure you're quite cramped here, and I must confess that I am chilled to the bone.'

We quickly ascended the stairs. Holmes threw off his cloak and briefly sojourned to his room to change into a dry shirt. When he returned, his piercing gaze fixed itself on me immediately.

'So, what is it?'

His voice had taken on a softer and gentler quality than I'd ever imagined could be possible for him.

I opened my mouth to speak, yet hesitated. Was I doing the right thing? *Yes,* I told myself sternly.

'I confess that I lied to you, and I cannot blame you in the slightest if you do not feel you can continue to help me after this.'

Holmes' brow crinkled in confusion.

'Claude Joseph Vernet was your great-great-great uncle.'

This time, the shock that lit up Holmes' face was as bright as day. His voice suddenly dropped as he leaned closer to me in an urgent manner. 'However did you know that?'

'Moriarty told me.'

'Today?'

I shook my head, chestnut-brown curls falling in my face.

'When?'

'When Ariana and I met him in the passageway and he revealed that he stole the painting. He submitted the tip that lost him his professorship. It was all to attract your attention.'

I paused briefly before forcing out the words I'd been almost too afraid to think.

'Even kidnapping Ariana – I don't think it was simply because she knew too much. He let Ariana find out about our brother. He let her lead me here. He could have easily silenced us both. But he knew that you would not be able to ignore a case if a relative of Doctor Watson's came about her sister's abduction.'

Holmes sucked in a long breath. 'Why did you not say anything before?'

I dropped my head again. 'I admit that I was foolish. I wanted this to only be about what he had done to me. I did not consider that even though I had obtained help, I might be putting those I had enlisted in needless danger. Until today.'

The detective studied me in silence for a moment. 'Thank you for telling me. Now you had best get up to bed; it is after midnight.'

I glanced up at the clock and realised for the first time that the great hands were indeed pointing to nearly half past twelve.

'I'm not tired,' I replied hollowly. Holmes did not protest.

'Why would getting himself fired attract my attention? The papers did not even mention his name.'

'It left him free to return to London and set his sights on you.'

'I found out tonight why Moriarty needed your stepfather's help,' Holmes said after a moment of pensive silence.

My head snapped up. 'You did?'

He stretched out his legs and made a large show of repositioning himself before replying.

'Peter Ashford – then known as Peter Moriarty – obtained a law degree from Cambridge University in 1863. He moved back to his home afterward. As far as I can tell, he only took on two cases after being admitted to the Suffolk County Bar.

'The first was to make up the last will and testament of an elderly man who lived alone on an estate outside a small town. He had no family whatsoever, so in return for your stepfather's help, he left Peter his house, as well as a considerable amount of money.'

'Thorndon Hall,' I breathed.

'Precisely. The second and final case he took was a deeply personal one. One James Moriarty, then in University himself, was accused of first-degree murder. He had allegedly poisoned a fellow student with a heavy dose of arsenic "to study its effects in comparison to normal levels." The family hired Moriarty's own brother for the defence.'

My jaw fell open. 'How on earth was that allowed? It's an obscene conflict of interest!'

'Everyone has a price, Emily. Moriarty was cleared of all charges, despite all but confessing to the crime in court, and the records were hidden well. I've been on quite the hunt this past week to find evidence of what occurred. I am most aggrieved to say that this information can only be for your ears and mine, for I lost the records I found when I took my unanticipated swim.

'All that to say, the week after the case was closed, Peter Ashford resigned from the Bar and filed the paperwork to change his name. Moriarty must have come to him for legal advice.'

I hid my shaking hands in the folds of my skirts. 'I appreciate all you have done to get this information,' I said quietly. 'I do think I should like to go to bed now.'

I rose, but Holmes stopped me. 'We will make this an effort between us.'

I nodded wearily and forced myself along the hallway to my bedroom. I was glad to have come clean, as well as to have this new knowledge, but I felt sick with the enormity of Moriarty's turpitude. It felt like colliding with a tidal wave.

We would capture Moriarty. We had to. He had gotten away with far too much.

Chapter 12: Power in Trust

'All empire is no more than power in trust.'
– John Dryden

Two more weeks went by, yet yielded no results – at least as far as I knew.

I watched Holmes' clients come and go from a distance, asked not to present myself to them as they likely did not know who I was, nor would they be as forthright in front of me.

I suspected that was not all there was. My inclination was that the genius detective separated me from his business because there was a measure of danger present. From what I could tell, Holmes greatly respected me and my desire to avenge myself upon Moriarty, but did not want to put me in extra jeopardy.

It was comforting, at least, that he did not doubt my capabilities.

After heavily discussing it, the two of us had decided to merely tell John that Holmes had uncovered no leads pertaining to my stepfather's murderer and that we had handed over the case to the police, as Holmes had too many other clients.

On the 4th of September, the Great Detective was engaged in a chemical experiment of some sort, filling the room with rancid smoke. My brother had entered, waving a hand in front of his face on the way to open a window.

'Holmes, when I said you fill my head, this is far from what I meant!'

In an attempt to clear my lungs, I was preparing to go out for a walk in the nearby Regent's Park. The weather was cool, so I pulled on a fleece-lined cloak. Mrs Hudson had quickly seen to it that my wardrobe was updated to fit the city's mercurial weather.

Upon descending the front steps, I was almost immediately approached by a crisply-dressed man with cropped dark hair and a rather blunted face. He couldn't have been over the age of thirty.

'Excuse me, miss, would that be number 221 you just left?' He spoke with a strong accent that I recognized as Russian, seeming quite frightened and speaking anxiously.

'Why yes,' I replied cautiously. 'Were you looking for it, sir?'

'I am, miss. It is the residence of Sherlock Holmes, yes?'

I nodded in confirmation.

'May I come in, then? I have found myself in a terrible situation.'

'Certainly. I will show you up to the sitting room, Mr...'

'Koval. My name is Dmitri Koval.'

I re-entered 221B to show our visitor to the sitting room where Holmes was excitedly bent over the acid-stained table. The smoke had thankfully dissipated.

I announced the client whose hands, I observed, were twitching nervously and slick with sweat as they toyed with his tie.

Holmes straightened and swept over to shake the man's hand jovially. 'Good afternoon, Mr Koval. I am Sherlock Holmes, and this is my loyal friend and associate, Doctor Watson. Beside you is the doctor's sister, Miss Emily, whom I see has shown you up. You are a political aide?'

My observational powers were strong, but I confess I had no idea how Holmes had deduced such a thing.

Apparently, neither did Koval.

'Mr Holmes, how in the world did you know that?'

'Your tie and shoes, of course!'

'Do not mind him, Mr Koval,' advised John. 'He quite enjoys showing off. Pray, take a seat. Why have you come?'

I was turning to leave when Holmes stopped me. 'Emily, please stay, if you would not mind. You brought this gentleman to us. You have earned the privilege of learning the particulars.'

Rather flustered by this, I shakily consented and took a seat beside my brother.

'I must ask you three to agree to let nothing I have said leave this room,' said Mr Koval, fingering his tie once more.

'I can assure you that we are not in the habit of breaking our promise of confidentiality,' Holmes assured him smoothly, my brother and myself nodding in agreement.

The man nodded. 'Good. The matter is of quite the delicate political nature. I'm afraid if word of it got out, it could very well cause a war.'

I drew back slightly, alarmed at the gravity of the situation.

Our client drew a deep, calming breath before beginning his tale. 'I am here from St. Petersburg as an aide to the renowned Russian statesman Alexei Ivanov. We were sent in an attempt to establish a peaceful liaison with your government. However, the visit has taken a terrible turn as of this morning.'

'How so?' asked Holmes, leaning forward.

'Mr Ivanov has been kidnapped.'

The detective leapt up and began to pace, much as he did the day he met me. 'What time did you find this to be so?'

'About eight o'clock this morning. When I came downstairs to collect my mail from the concierge desk, there was an incredibly eccentric and anonymous note among them, appearing to follow some sort of code, asking for a ransom. It alarmed me very much, so I got a spare key for Mr Ivanov's room from the desk. When I went in, I discovered the room was empty. There were no signs of a struggle. And there is no word of him arriving at the Foreign Office this morning.'

'And have you gone to the police? They would be more prepared to deal with this delicate matter than I.'

'They would not look into it,' said Koval, shaking his head. 'They said that the note must surely be a joke of some kind, and that since everything in his room was in place, Mr Ivanov must have merely gone out somewhere in the city.'

Holmes nodded thoughtfully. 'We must accept this as a possibility, I am afraid. It is possible that the note is a hoax only intended to extort money. May I see it?'

'Of course.'

From his inside coat pocket, Koval drew a plain envelope, addressed in block letters to one Dmitri Koval of Room 214 at the Northumberland Hotel. Holmes studied it intently before opening it to peruse the contents.

'Is the entire note in block lettering?' I asked.

'I am afraid so,' said Holmes regretfully. 'There is nothing to be deduced from the writing itself. The paper is the hotel's own stationery, and the language used in the note is quite… nonsensical.'

'Read it out loud. Perhaps we could make something of it together.'

Holmes cleared his throat and began to read:

Fifteen men on the dead man's chest—
Yo-ho-ho, and a bottle of rum!
Drink and the devil had done for the rest—
Yo-ho-ho, and a bottle of rum!
Admiral Benbow has the answers at best—
Yo-ho-ho, and a bottle of rum!
The treasure you'll give me to add to my nest—
Yo-ho-ho, and a bottle of rum!
Search for my name on my very own crest—
Yo-ho-ho, and a bottle of rum!
I'll bet you can't find me before the inquest—
Yo-ho-ho, and a bottle of rum!
And if you bring help, I'll kill my dear guest—
Yo-ho-ho, and a bottle of rum!
Good luck and good day, and may you be blessed—
Yo-ho-ho, and a bottle of rum!

My stomach lurched as I recognised the first four lines.

On the other hand, my brother certainly hadn't. 'May I ask who in the world Admiral Benbow is?'

A modern adventure story, a tale of pirates and treasure – of course most grown men had not read it.

Yet, that was not what twisted my stomach into knots.

I had been reading this very book in the library at Thorndon Hall just three weeks ago. It all felt like a terrible coincidence.

I swallowed my nerves and spoke. 'Actually, Admiral Benbow is the name of an inn. That and the first four lines of the note are taken straight from Robert Louis Stevenson's *Treasure Island*.'

'Are you saying that we must go to this inn for the answers?' Holmes's eyebrows were raised sceptically.

'That isn't possible, I'm afraid. The inn is a fictional location. I believe the author of this note intended it to mean that the answer lies in the story of *Treasure Island* itself. And since no one else here appears to have read it… Perhaps I can be of assistance on the case.'

Simply to lend a hand and a ready mind, I tried to convince myself, *and not at all because I have a grave suspicion about where this might lead.*

Sighing, I rearranged my skirts for what felt like the millionth time as I recalled Holmes's instructions. My job was to alert the police of the matter concerning the disappearance of Mr Ivanov, then make my way to the Northumberland Hotel. There, I was to question the hotel concierge whom Koval had told us was on duty when the ransom note was delivered.

A glance at the wall clock, which seemed to mock my idle mind with each repetitive *tick-tock,* revealed that I had been waiting in the Commissioner's Office for nearly three quarters of an hour. I sat politely on the settee the meek and petite young secretary had shown me to, but I was getting far too restless. I wanted to know more about Chief Commissioner Lynch.

Unable to control my limbs anymore, I found myself standing up and walking over to the cluttered desk. A lead bust of the former Prime Minister Benjamin Disraeli was being used as a paperweight, holding down a thick stack of official-looking documents. I picked it up and skimmed some of the papers.

'I do not wish to impose upon your Majesty's evening, but the situation is really quite desperate,' read one of the pieces on top. It was written in a minuscule, hurried script, and appeared to be a discarded draft of a letter to Her Majesty Queen Victoria.

I would have perused further, but I really had no idea how much longer I had before Lynch arrived. With another quick look at the time, I tugged on one of the desk drawers. Of course, it was locked.

The next one, however, opened under my touch. It was filled with what looked to be outdated parliamentary debates and a gun. *How odd,* I thought, *why would* this *drawer be unlocked?*

As I frowned at the mystery, the office door suddenly opened. I immediately shot to my feet, heart pounding in the back of my throat.

In the doorway stood a fair-skinned, dark-haired boy of average height. His arms were crossed, head tilted to one side, staring at me through narrowed eyes. 'I'm sure I have no desire to know what you're doing.'

While I did not know who this boy was, I had more than a sneaking suspicion that he could easily get me into trouble.

'I was just—'

The boy held up a hand. 'No need.' He stepped forward and extended his hand. 'Andrew Lynch. And you are?'

'Emily Watson.'

Andrew Lynch lifted my hand and kissed it. 'I trust you are here to see my father, Miss Watson?'

'I am,' I nodded.

'Well, I cannot help but wonder what sort of errand might cause you to come here. Outside of my father's secretary, I have never known any woman to enter this room.'

I cocked my head, a ghost of a smile playing at the corners of my mouth. 'You ask a lot of questions.'

'Do I not get any answers from you?'

'That was another question. And I do not believe my business is any of yours.'

Andrew's face held an expression of mock offence, but his voice betrayed that he was perhaps a little impressed. 'Well, you're rather full of spunk.'

I adjusted my hat, staring him straight in the eye. 'It's how I get what I want. Now it's my turn to ask a question or two.'

Andrew straightened his posture, waiting, as if he were under a Commander's scrutiny. It was quite amusing.

'Does the Chief Commissioner's son often loiter around Scotland Yard?'

'I am not loitering, Miss Watson, I am helping my father.'

'And how do the officers take to that?'

'You have not answered my questions, why should I oblige?'

'Ah, so not well at all. Intriguing as that is, I do have one more inquiry that does not pertain to you.'

His eyes glinted and I got the sense that he did not want me to get to the point of my visit.

'Will I be able to see your father today or should I come back? I do have pressing business elsewhere.'

'It depends. How pressing are these matters?'

'A life could hang in the balance.'

'Well then, I suggest that you take care of that first and come back tomorrow. My father should be in after half past two.'

I nodded and headed towards the door. 'Thank you.'

Andrew intercepted me. 'Wait. Who sent you here?'

'Mr Sherlock Holmes.'

Andrew's face showed disbelief. Using it as leverage, I wished him a good day and walked briskly down the hallway.

I could pick out the massive hotel the moment I stepped out of the cab. It stood out boldly from the nondescript buildings along Euston Road.

My eyes widened when I stepped inside the elaborate lobby. Marble tile gleamed from beneath my feet, perfectly reflecting the shimmering chandeliers hung from the ceiling.

The concierge at the desk looked up right away when he noticed I had stepped in. 'Can I help you, miss?' he asked, closing the ledger that he was updating.

'Yes, I'm looking for Mr Lambert. Would you happen to know where he is?'

'I haven't seen him all day, ma'am. Maybe I can help you?'

I shook my head vehemently. 'I must insist that I speak with Mr Lambert directly.'

The concierge looked uncomfortable.

'I can't leave my post, ma'am, but you could check the employee's lounge down this hallway here.' He gestured at a hall entrance behind him. I made my way behind the desk and toward the lounge. I immediately stopped once I stepped inside.

A man with a bronze name tag reading Lambert was lying in the middle of the floor, face up, frozen in surprise. Blood was spreading in a circle from under his head.

I kneeled and reached down to touch Lambert's wrist. His skin was still warm.

Why here? Why now?

I stood up and struggled not to run as I turned out of the room and straight into the concierge from the desk who had apparently been curious enough to leave his post after all.

I glanced at his name tag. 'Mr McAllister, would you happen to have a telephone I could use?'

Chapter 13: Be Bold

> *'How over that same door was likewise writ,*
> *Be bold, be bold, and everywhere Be bold.*
> *... Another iron door, on which was writ,*
> *Be not too bold.'*
>   – *Edmund Spenser*

'You were the one to discover the body?'

I barely heard the police inspector's inquiry. I was too busy attempting to peer into the room where Lambert's body lay exactly as I had found it.

There was something dreadfully familiar about the entire scenario. My mind recalled images of another man lying still in a pool of blood, killed with a single gunshot to the head.

Sir Peter Ashford. My stepfather.

The only difference here was that there was no open window. The bullet's origin had clearly been inside the room.

'Miss?'

I started, broken out of my train of thought. 'Excuse me?'

'Did you find the body?' the inspector asked again, pencil poised over his notebook.

'Oh. Yes, I did.'

The man, who had cordially introduced himself as Inspector Gregson, nodded briskly and scribbled down my response with incredible ferocity. He then fixed his blue-eyed gaze on me again. 'Miss, if you would please head towards the lobby so we can commence our investigation. We will come find you if we require anything else.'

I opened my mouth to explain what precisely I was doing there when Inspector Lestrade appeared in the hallway. His tense posture and gasping breath betrayed that he was embarrassingly late.

'Gregson, let her be. This young woman is acquainted with Mr Holmes and the doctor.'

'Don't be so preposterous, Lestrade, she's only a girl. Not even fifteen years of age.'

'Actually, I'm sixteen,' I interjected coldly.

Gregson stared at me, not quite sure what to make of my bold interruption of their conversation.

Lestrade moved closer, practically pushing the other inspector aside. 'Now, Mr Holmes has stopped to question the members of the hotel staff. He and the doctor will be along directly. If you do not mind, Miss Emily, I would like to speak with you alone.' He gently took my arm and guided me down the corridor. 'I did manage to speak to Mr Holmes for a couple of minutes when I arrived. He informs me of the reason you were sent here. I understand that the dead man was personally given the ransom note and instructed to pass it on to Mr Koval?'

I nodded, crossing my arms and looking around us uncomfortably. 'There's something else.'

Lestrade nodded.

'You've seen the photographs from my stepfather's study, haven't you?'

'I have.'

'Well, the scene here reminds me very much of his death. It isn't like a normal crime scene. It's far too neat.'

'And how many crime scenes have you personally seen, Miss Emily?'

I averted my gaze. 'Not many. But I am almost positive that they are far more chaotic than this. In case you haven't noticed, the only real evidence is the body.'

'You think the same person was responsible.'

'Yes.'

Lestrade sighed. 'This man, Moriarty, might be running an underground criminal syndicate, but that does not mean he's behind every crime in London. You're seeing him everywhere, Emily. It's common, believe me. But don't worry.'

'Inspector, did Holmes tell you about the ransom note?'

'He did inform me of it, yes.'

'I have a very intuitive feeling that it was meant to attract my attention. It was taken from the very book I was reading the day that Moriarty arrived in Thorndon.'

'And tell me, how could he have known what you were reading before you even met him?'

'He has my sister. God only knows what he's forced out of her.'

Lestrade tightened his lips grimly. 'I am sorry, Miss Emily, but professionally, I cannot allow myself to be persuaded until we find evidence that proves your theory.'

I let out a frustrated breath. How could I be the only one who saw how cleanly the pieces fit together?

I took off my hat and ran a hand through my carefully pinned up hair, allowing a few strands to fall loose from their clips. Turning around, I scanned the small crowd of police officers who were weaving back and forth, comparing notes and examining – but not moving – anything that might be evidence. Amid the organised chaos, I saw Holmes and John making their way purposefully in my direction.

'Gregson!' The detective bellowed, clapping the man on the shoulder as he passed. 'Lestrade was kind enough to accompany us on a search of Ivanov's hotel room, so do not sink to the level of criticising his lateness.'

'Did you find anything of use, sir?' Gregson asked hopefully.

'Ivanov was indeed taken from his hotel room. There are traces of multiple pairs of shoes on the carpeting. Not just Koval's from his initial entry, either. When he came to us today, I observed his peculiar shoes – they are by a certain Russian cobbler who only sells to a political clientele. These tracks were various and different, at least two pairs aside from the two we can identify. However, despite the forceful presence in his room, Ivanov left willingly. I'd wager he has some stake in all of this.'

'Are you all right?' asked my brother, taking me tenderly by the shoulder, his deep brown eyes filled with concern.

I glanced quickly over his shoulder. Holmes was already busy with the scene, though I could no longer hear whatever deductions he was making. He waved his hand dismissively at something and continued through the room, brushing past anyone who stood in his way to kneel near the body.

'I'm perfectly fine,' I said, meeting John's gaze. 'I have seen dead bodies before, as you are aware.'

'Good. Now, my presence is most likely needed in there, so...' He began to walk away, but then turned and held up a firm hand in my direction before getting lost in the wave of officers. 'Stay here.'

I rolled my eyes and slouched against the wall. *What the devil was I doing?* This body pertained to a case that Holmes was allowing me to help with. It was only fair that I was present.

And what if there was some other piece of evidence in there? Since it was obvious that this was connected to Ivanov's disappearance, it might pertain to *Treasure Island*. In that case, I was the only one who would be able to decipher it.

I waited until Gregson's back was turned before silently slipping past two constables arguing how to archive a police statement.

Holmes was examining the room, standing so close to the far wall that his nose was almost pressing against it. Lestrade was standing a couple of feet back, arms crossed and watching his actions with intense interest. He must have noticed me out of the corner of his eye, for he turned and winked at me. I crossed the room, my line of sight inevitably falling on the body. John was busy examining the eyes and hands.

'Doctor Watson told me he instructed you to stay in the hall,' murmured Lestrade, his gaze flitting between Holmes and my brother.

'I can help you. There might be a clue in here alluding to *Treasure Island* and without me, you'd completely overlook it.'

The inspector raised a hand to massage the back of his neck, biting his lip in uncertainty, but agreed to let me stay.

When Holmes finished examining the wall, he turned to speak to Lestrade, finding him with me. 'Emily!'

On hearing my name, John started and looked up. 'I specifically told you to stay outside!'

'You need my help.' I was practically pleading.

That's when I noticed it.

The area of flooring around the body had a different outline compared to the rest. It seemed to be a square all of its own.

'Can we move the body?' I asked urgently, kneeling beside the seam in the wood.

'Doctor?' Lestrade inquired.

My brother caressed his moustache thoughtfully. 'Only if it is concealing vital evidence.'

I nodded. 'Then we need to move him to the side. Haven't you noticed he's lying on top of a trapdoor?'

Holmes' eyes travelled to the floor as if for the first time.

Lestrade gaped at him. 'You could've told us, eh, Holmes?'

The detective looked sheepish. 'I glanced at the body, but I was saving the floor for last. I find it's always best to search a room from the ceiling down.'

'Or from the floor up,' I argued with a cocked eyebrow. 'You might very well tread on a clue, looking up at the stars.'

Lestrade rolled his eyes and called a couple of the officers around him. 'McFarlane, Kingston, help the doctor move the body!' he barked at the two constables I'd passed on the way in.

They quickly hoisted the body and set it down nearer to the opposite wall according to John's instructions.

Much of the blood had pooled around the head and shoulders. But there was a trapdoor visible, the latch coated in sticky red liquid. Gregson had entered the room out of curiosity; he now stood watching with us as Lestrade knelt to open the door.

'Third pair of ruined trousers in the last month,' the inspector muttered under his breath as he wiped the blood off his hands. 'My salary can't pay for all this!'

The latch lifted to reveal a single box about the size of a travel trunk. Both Lestrade's and Holmes' best efforts were needed to lift it out of the hole.

'Why exactly is there a trapdoor in the Employee's Lounge?' asked my brother, mystified.

'I worked here when I was young,' one of the nameless officers piped up. 'We were told some handy bellhop had made it long ago for a secret stash of liquor.'

Lestrade groaned. 'I wish there was still liquor in there. I could use a pint, or four.'

'Come now, old friend, this isn't the time to bemoan your alcoholism,' Holmes said lightly as he examined the lock. 'Certainly it will require a key.'

I massaged my head. It appeared a clever scavenger hunt had been prepared for us. 'Have you checked Lambert's pockets?'

Holmes cackled buoyantly. 'The body was face-up! A shot in the back of the head would have felled him face-first, unless, of course, he was turned over so that a clue could be planted on his person.'

Lestrade's eyes held a spark, but this time Gregson made sure he was the first to speak. I sensed a strong rivalry between the two inspectors, and if the apprehension of the officers was any indication, it had prevented them from being assigned together in quite some time.

'Kingston, search his pockets.'

As the officer's hand plunged into the dead man's breast pocket, his face lit up, extracting a worn bronze object.

Lestrade promptly snatched the key from him. 'Emily, please do the honours. I feel I owe you something for not believing you at first.'

John glanced up at us, eyes narrowed. 'Not believing you about what?'

'That there would be more clues pertaining to *Treasure Island*,' I answered quickly. I accepted the key gratefully, inserting it into the lock in a clockwise motion.

The lid sprang open.

At first glance, the box appeared to be empty.

Then I looked at the bottom and saw a scroll of paper and a small, wooden box.

Holmes picked up the paper and unrolled it, revealing a world map. I opened the box, discovering eight silver coins.

'Pieces of eight.'

Each one had a view of a different city, the name labelled on a scroll at the bottom. London, England. Bern, Switzerland. Madrid, Spain. Belfast, Ireland. Oslo, Norway. Rome, Italy. Reykjavik, Iceland. Rabat, Morocco.

I looked at the map which Holmes held before him.

'There's an inscription at the bottom,' he informed us.

'What does it say?' asked Gregson.

'X marks the spot.'

Suddenly, I had an idea.

'Holmes, lay that map down on the floor. Over here, where there's no blood.'

Once he did, I set to work matching the cities on the coins to their respective locations on the map. Soon, I found that the eight markers made up the image of a lopsided X.

'But what does that mean?' asked Lestrade.

'The centre point of the X is London,' I explained. 'Therefore, the so-called treasure we seek is here.'

Holmes bent over the map as I stood, as though it betrayed all the secrets of the universe.

And perhaps, to him, it did.

Looking around me, I saw a familiar face in the doorway.

'Hello, Mr Lynch,' I greeted.

'Miss Watson,' he nodded at me casually as he leaned against the door frame. 'What might you be doing here?'

'I could ask you the same thing.'

'My father brought me along to observe, but we had barely arrived when he was called away to meet with the Prime Minister. Your turn.'

'This is where I needed to be after meeting your father. I had an urgent matter in which I needed the dead man's help.'

'So that's what you meant when you said that a life could hang in the balance.'

I very nearly blushed because he remembered my words, before remembering that it hadn't even been two hours ago.

'Actually, I wasn't talking about him,' I said as we stepped into the hall together. 'I meant the diplomat Alexei Ivanov, who has been kidnapped, as you may know. Ivanov's aide hired Holmes to find him. Mr Lambert may have had crucial information as to his whereabouts.'

'My father mentioned the case being brought in by the aide this morning,' replied Andrew as we began to stroll back towards the lobby. He was perfectly calm, as if we were discussing the results of the week's cricket matches. 'He could not allow resources to be wasted on it right away. He said there were too many variables.'

'Yes, because the room had not been at all disturbed.'

Andrew nodded. 'And there was every possibility that the note was merely the work of a prankster, or an extortionist.'

I caught his eye seriously. 'I hope no one is still convinced of that. People aren't shot in the head for pranks.'

We entered the lobby and were immediately accosted by McAllister, the man who had been at the concierge desk when I first came in.

'Miss Watson?'

'Yes?'

'This was just dropped off for you at the desk.' He held out a plain envelope.

'Thank you,' I replied with a nod and swiftly broke the seal with my fingernail. Inside was a single sheet of foolscap paper. The few words written in thin, spidery script which was all too familiar to me:

My dear Emily,
You have fallen into the trap I set for you. Going any further will only put you in unnecessary danger. I implore you to let it go.
Sincerely,
J. M.

'Mr McAllister, who gave you this?'

'A short, skinny man, red hair and a small scar on his cheek. He just left.' He nodded at the door, towards which I turned sharply.

Andrew, out of curiosity, followed my gaze.

The door was still swinging slightly on its hinges. I could just see a head of flaming red hair disappear into the crowd. It could not have been Moriarty, but it was certainly someone in his employ.

Which meant I was right.
I was beginning to hate being right.

Chapter 14: The Art of War

'The art of war is of vital importance to the State. It is a matter of life and death, a road either to safety or to ruin. Hence it is a subject of inquiry which can on no account be neglected.'
– Sun Tzu

Andrew stared at my face worriedly.

'Emily, are you all right?' he asked, guiding me to a settee as the blood drained from my face.

I took a gulp of air and breathed deeply before answering, surprisingly not bothered by his use of my first name. 'Yes, I'm fine.'

'What is in that letter? Who is it from?'

I had no idea what made me do it, but I sank forward with my head in my hands and allowed Andrew to take the note from my loose grasp.

'Who is *J. M.*?'

'His name is James Moriarty. He's the former Professor of Mathematics at the University of St. Andrews. He is my stepfather's brother, and...' I trailed off, nearly choking on the massive lump in my throat.

'And?' prompted Andrew Lynch gently.

I took another steadying breath. 'And he killed him.'

'He killed your stepfather?'

I merely nodded. Everything inside my head was so terribly jumbled. Why on earth was I detailing the nature of a confidential case to a boy I'd only met today?

There was something that made me believe that he could keep a secret forever. And he was the son of a high-ranking police official.

I decided to keep talking. It felt rather good. 'He also kidnapped my sister. I know what she knows, so now he's after me as well.'

Even though I was still hiding my face, I could picture Andrew's lips tightening. I felt the cushion of the settee pressing flat as he leaned back.

'Let me guess, you came to London to ask for Holmes's help.'

Again, I nodded.

'Why didn't you bring this to the police first? Holmes is only an amateur. Scotland Yard can give you protection.'

'When I arrived, I didn't even know Holmes lived at Baker Street. All I knew was that my half-brother was there. I couldn't stay at my stepfather's estate and risk being in even worse danger. I was concerned with finding the only family I had left, not notifying the police.'

'But why didn't you come to us after you settled at Baker Street?' He spoke as if he were himself an official member of the Force.

Finally, I made eye contact with the boy. I noticed for the first time how his sapphire-blue eyes seemed to sparkle in the light. He wasn't bothered by his dark brown, shaggy hair falling over his left eye.

I tore myself away from his more engaging physical qualities before I lost my focus.

'Because Moriarty is running a criminal organisation. He only eludes the police because he most probably has his own agents within their ranks. We do not know who among the officers of Scotland Yard is really employed by a more sinister force.'

Andrew was silent for a moment before replying, his voice barely above a whisper. 'So why are you telling me?'

There it was. The question I could not answer. It was as if some invisible lever was controlling my mouth. I began to stutter, finally getting out a full coherent sentence.

'I...I don't know.'

Shame reddened my cheeks. I childishly buried my face in my hands once again. Andrew placed a steady, yet tender hand on my right shoulder.

I was truly shocked that I didn't move away from it.

Was this the beginning of a romantic attachment? I couldn't be sure, for I had never experienced such a thing before.

I didn't know what to make of it. Any idea that I'd had of what love was had died with my mother, and any remnants of that had disappeared with Ariana. This left me with no idea how to process emotions like this, and being rather uncomfortable with the prospect.

And yet, I let his supportive hand remain where it was.

The next evening following dinner, John went out to his regular officer's club, leaving Holmes and I alone at 221B.

I was perusing the *Evening News* when Holmes bounded up the stairs, tossing my waterproof cloak into my lap. He was already wearing his Inverness.

'Where are we going?'

'Pall Mall.'

'Is there a reason we need to go there in this weather?' I asked, jerking my head in the direction of the window.

'My brother lives there.'

I stopped. 'You have a brother?'

'Yes, Mycroft. He is seven years my senior and works in Whitehall, auditing government books. Or so he claims. He is an influential part of many departments. In fact, there are occasions when he *is* the British Government.'

Mouth agape, I obediently slipped on my cloak and followed downstairs. Holmes held me back inside while he hailed a cab.

The ride was silent for the most part until we passed through Grosvenor Square. Only then did I catch Holmes' eye.

'Have you made any progress on the Moriarty case?' I asked him. Christ willing, I didn't sound too hopeful.

'I have been spending a good deal of time in Scotland Yard's archives, pulling files of crimes never completely closed, which may have some bearing on his organisation.'

'But do we have a man inside the group itself?'

He shifted his weight and met my gaze earnestly. 'Emily, in all probability, that will take years. The agent could never be accepted right away. He'll have to ease his way into Moriarty's trust. And as for his possible connection to Ivanov's disappearance… As Lestrade told you, there's no definite proof.'

I felt a knot form in my stomach as I realised that I had never shown him the note from yesterday.

'Actually, I have to show you something that might help to prove just that.' I reached deep into my pocket to pull out the envelope. I didn't dare leave without it.

Holmes cleared his throat upon reading the thinly-veiled threat and fixed me with a gaze so serious it sent chills down my spine. 'When did you get this?'

'Yesterday, at the crime scene. McAllister from the concierge desk gave it to me. He said a short man with red hair and a scar on his cheek had delivered it. The man in question had just left when I got to the lobby.'

Holmes placed the letter on the seat beside him and leaned forward, his expression still grim. 'Emily, this is nothing to Moriarty. Killing his own blood, causing chaos among the official ranks – it's all an equation to his mind. There are many things that are imbalances. They will be eliminated at all costs. We are all his pawns in a very dangerous game. Do you understand this?'

I nodded numbly, unsure what to reply.

'So, you understand that you need to step back and keep yourself as far away from the danger as possible?'

No. He knew that I was planning to find Ariana myself and he had done nothing to hold me back before. Why now?

I was not going to back out.

'What difference will that make? It's what I know that makes me a danger to his equation. I can't simply forget. I'll be in danger either way.'

'All I must do is put in a word with Lestrade and you'll have protection. We won't let him get to you.'

'You said it's almost certain he has men in the police force.'

'So Lestrade and I will vet them together. You think I am not serious? Doctor John Watson is the best man I have ever known. No relative of his will come to any harm if I have any say in the matter.'

He was very adamant. I decided to back off for now. I might not be giving up, but I didn't need to let Holmes know that. Putting on my best uncertain face, I averted my gaze for a moment before looking back at him, filling my eyes with the fear that I truly felt.

'All right, I'll let it go. I promise.'

He nodded his approval, but I wasn't finished.

'But can I please do what I can to help you find Mr Ivanov? I promise not to get involved as far as Moriarty goes.'

Holmes thought for a moment, fingering the edges of the envelope beside him. 'I suppose it couldn't do any harm. In fact, Alexei Ivanov's disappearance is why we are going to Mycroft.'

'What connection would he have to all this?'

'My brother has many useful contacts within the Foreign Office,' said Holmes as our cab pulled up to a nondescript brick building. 'As I explained, he deals with virtually every part of the government.'

He leapt out of the cab to offer me a hand down. I accepted, shivering as the icy cold raindrops began attacking me at once, stinging like the impact of a thousand frozen knives.

We entered the building, which I was surprised to discover was far more sophisticated than Baker Street, although it looked almost identical on the outside. The walls were a deep red, covered with stripes that tapered off into spirals at the ceiling and floor. Polished bronze gas lamps were installed all around the room, and the carpet appeared to be of authentic Persian origin. There was a luxurious velvet chair and a table made of deep brown cherry wood by a set of stairs.

A young maid not much older than myself timidly took our wet cloaks and showed us up the stairs.

'This house is quite... impressive,' I murmured to Holmes as we ascended the staircase.

'Indeed. The British Government pays a fine sum for Mycroft's position.'

We entered a sitting room just as elegant as the downstairs. A very tall, portly man had opened the door for us. He was clean-shaven, but his suit jacket and tie were off. In his hands, he clutched a respectably thick file of papers.

'Sherlock,' Mycroft greeted his younger brother cordially, clapping him on the shoulder. 'Ah, this is the sister of the good doctor, then?' He took my hand. 'A pleasure, Miss Watson.'

Sherlock's brother directed us to a couple of armchairs by the fireplace. I sat down on one with Holmes beside me.

I wondered how many visitors the elder Holmes regularly received. If he was such an important man, why did he not take them in his office?

'It was quite the unintelligent move by Scotland Yard to ignore the case concerning Alexei Ivanov when it was offered to them on a silver platter,' said Mycroft, sinking down wearily into the chair across from us.

I wrinkled my brow, leaning in towards Holmes. 'You told him why we were coming?'

'Not a word.'

'So I am correct in my deduction.'

Holmes met my eye. 'I must have forgotten to mention it, but my brother possesses deductive capabilities even greater than my own.'

The elder Holmes snorted. 'Please, Sherlock. If I were a better reasoner than you, I would be the one who elected to become a detective. I do not deduce the things I know. As you and I are both aware, I have far more... tangible sources than thought alone. Now, why have you come to me about Ivanov?'

'His aide, as you have *deduced*, came to me yesterday. He said that he had received the ransom note and had Ivanov's room checked at approximately eight in the morning. Mr Koval had inquired at the Foreign Office, but there had been no sign of him. As you said, the police refused to investigate the case until there was more substantial proof that the man had been abducted.'

Mycroft leaned back in his chair, alarmingly nonchalant. I supposed by now that this attitude ran in the family.

'I met with Mr Ivanov earlier this week. It was the day he and his aide, Mr Koval, arrived, to be precise. In an official capacity, the Russian representative was sent by some of the more peaceful liberals in Imperial Russia to form a liaison between the nations to resolve the childish squabbles over land in Central Asia.

'On a completely different level, however, I am afraid that my department of the Foreign Office has discovered evidence suggesting that Ivanov has ties to a number of Russian Revolutionary groups, many of which are harboured here.'

'But considering recent relations between ourselves and the Russian Imperial Government, wouldn't an Imperialist associating with Revolutionaries be good news for our cause?' I asked. I knew just enough about foreign affairs to understand what he was saying. The Revolutionaries were, after all, being harboured in London for a reason. Any enemy of the Russian Imperials was, in some capacity, a friend of the British.

Mycroft sighed and turned his gaze to me. 'While the knowledge could certainly be used to our advantage, the British Government is even more concerned with security than we are with land. If we kept it to ourselves, we could very well use it to regain the favour of the Imperialists, but all the same, what Ivanov was doing was treason. It would be an enormous conflict of interest, not to mention a catalyst for outright war.'

I looked over at Holmes. His eyes were serious, and he sighed heavily, meeting my gaze.

'Emily, what my brother is trying to say is that some government officials are already convinced that the Russian government discovered Ivanov's involvement with the Revolutionaries and arranged for him to disappear.'

My head was spinning with this cornucopia of information.
'Did our government tell them about the Revolutionaries?'

'No, they did not, Miss Watson,' replied Mycroft sombrely. 'Only myself and the agent reporting to me knew.'

And suddenly I knew where this was inevitably headed. Meeting Holmes' gaze, I could tell that he knew as well.

'Mycroft is the most trustworthy man in the British Government, Emily. I have informed him of our little situation. Feel free to speak what's on your mind.'

Mycroft gestured with his head in agreement.

'I assume, then, that Moriarty somehow caught wind of it.'

Mycroft's eyebrows shot up in alarm and he held up a hand. 'Sherlock, are you insinuating that Moriarty is somehow involved in this? Is there something I do not know?'

The younger Holmes nodded and pulled my letter out of his pocket, handing it to his brother. 'While at the scene of Lambert's murder yesterday, Emily received this missive.'

The elder Holmes's eyebrows continued to raise as he read and reread the few lines of careful script.

'If Moriarty employed the use of his agents to uncover this information, he could have relayed it to the Imperialist Russians. They would then become convinced that we were withholding information from them, that we were scheming against them.

'They would also arrange for Ivanov, an apparent traitor, to mysteriously vanish. But they would not allow our government to find out about it – they would have us continue to believe that Ivanov had been abducted by terrorists; possibly have more ransom notes delivered – a sure way to con our government out of their money.'

'And the British Government would undoubtedly pay the ransom, convinced that they were keeping the information secret from the Russians for the safety of the Empire,' finished Holmes.

Surely, I thought, *Mycroft will alert the government of this?*

'What do we do with this information?'

Mycroft's eyes glinted in a way eerily like his brother's. 'We play our hand discreetly. We pay the ransom demand when it appears, then catch these agents in the act.'

The Great Detective smirked to show that he concurred with his brother's plan. 'And for now, we wait.'

Chapter 15: The Spider and the Fly

'He dragged her up his winding stair, into his dismal den,
Within his little parlour—but she ne'er came out again!
—And now, dear little children, who may this story read,
To idle, silly, flattering words, I pray you ne'er give heed:
Unto an evil counsellor, close heart, and ear, and eye,
And take a lesson from this tale, of the Spider and the Fly.'
    – Mary Howitt

I could not help but feel that I was a part of something special. It might not have been the best expression since a man was dead, another missing, and a criminal mastermind behind the underlying espionage and blackmail. But I suppose that for the first time, I felt as if I could do something of importance.

The next day, I awoke feeling anything but refreshed. I laid awake for hours, wondering how to work on the Moriarty case without Holmes' knowledge.

There was only one person who could help.

Finally, when I heard John ring Mrs Hudson for breakfast from down the hall, I rose and dressed, not bothering with my hair.

I joined my brother at the table, filling my plate with fried eggs, oatcakes and kippers. As I ate quietly, John informed me that Holmes had gone to alert Lestrade of the progress we had made.

After clearing my plate as hastily as possible, I cleared my throat. 'I'm going out.'

'And where, exactly, are you going? I would be remiss to let you wander London alone.'

'I'm not going to *wander London.*' I floundered momentarily for an excuse. 'Yesterday I noticed a bookseller in Manchester Square I wanted to visit.' *Not a lie.*

'Do you… need money?'

'No, thank you.'

I hoped it seemed obvious to John that I was done discussing my imminent departure. Fortunately, he seemed to take the hint, for he gave a brief nod.

I grabbed a cloak to protect myself from the chilled breeze and left for Scotland Yard. I would have to steer clear of Holmes and Lestrade, for I was going to see Andrew.

※

The challenge began the instant I entered the Metropolitan Police Headquarters. I walked through the doors just in time to witness the two men I had to avoid at all costs at the reception desk, talking animatedly. The room was not very crowded at all; they would notice me immediately.

Panicking, I dove behind a tall potted plant, peering through the somewhat sparse foliage at the two men. Holmes seemed to be looking directly at me…

In a moment, however, the men were presented with a key (perhaps for the archive rooms as the sign on the wall read) and they went on their way.

I let out an enormous breath, coming out from behind the large plant.

Standing right in my path was Andrew Lynch. His hands were on his hips, once again extremely amused at my antics.

'Andrew!' I jumped. 'What are you doing here?'

'Emily, don't pretend you didn't come here to see me. I am not an idiot.'

'I didn't think you were.' I stammered more than I should. 'What can I do for you?'

'I need to talk to you about what I said at the crime scene.'

Andrew's lips tightened. 'Emily, please. You must let me tell my father.'

'You can't. This information could fall into the wrong hands easier than you know.'

'Believe me when I say my father is not in league with a criminal mastermind.'

I dropped my voice to a hiss. 'He may not be, but odds are he works in close proximity to someone who is. The stakes are too high.'

'Such as? Holmes' opinion of you?'

'You may call Holmes a petty amateur, but remember that I associate with him every day. Trust me when I say that he knows what he's doing.'

'I've known him longer than you, I do believe.'

'You're not even an officer! You're the Commissioner's son who acts the part at crime scenes!'

I instantly regretted the harsh words, but Andrew seemed not at all ruffled. Indeed, he tilted his head curiously.

'My father is appearing in front of Parliament this morning. We can talk in his office.' He beckoned for me to follow him up several staircases until we reached the same room I had been waiting in just two days before.

It suddenly occurred to me that I had never actually met with Chief Commissioner Lynch. But the police now knew about Ivanov, so it was of no consequence.

It gave me a sense of satisfaction that I was working on the case in an official capacity while Scotland Yard had completely waived their opportunity to gain full privileges.

For some reason, I had expected Andrew, acting the part of an officer as he did, to take a seat behind his father's desk. It was a big chair to fill – in more ways than one – but I had no doubt he was capable. In my mind, he placed his elbows on the desk, hands clasped under his chin, and gave me a condescending look.

However, Andrew did none of those things. Instead, he sat down on the settee beside me. I was struck by the simple chivalry in the gesture. He was not trying to act self-important. He was simply there.

'So,' he said, shaking me out of my thoughts, 'what more did you need to say to me?'

Carefully, I recalled every word we'd exchanged at Mycroft's last night, not omitting a single detail. Andrew's eyes did not stray from my face once. They did not widen, nor did they narrow. The boy did not speak until I was finished.

'If you are so determined to orchestrate his fall, I would love to help you.'

I sighed. 'Andrew, I do not want to bring anyone else into this. But unfortunately, I need the help of someone who will not shield me or hamper my involvement.'

His blue eyes were filled with compassion and something akin to concern. 'I will not hamper your involvement, but I must admit, I am still not fond of you getting involved without any professional assistance. Emily, I—'

A sharp, precise knock on the office door interrupted his thought. None other than Inspector Lestrade and Sherlock Holmes stepped inside.

'Emily!' exclaimed Holmes while Lestrade yelped, 'Miss Watson!'

Andrew leaped out of his seat, face pale. He ran his hands through his shaggy hair. 'Would you be looking for my father, Inspector? He's out, you know.'

'I know, lad,' Lestrade replied dryly. 'Your father asked me to come by and pick up a file on Ivanov's career from his desk. He thought it might be helpful to Mr Holmes. Now, Emily, what in blazes are *you* doing here?'

'And alone with Lynch's bird-brained son!' added Holmes harshly.

Andrew averted his gaze. I had to defend his intelligence and disposition, although I didn't voice those thoughts.

'I don't think that's any concern of yours,' I bit back instead, pushing past Holmes. Shooting an apologetic glance at Andrew was all I could do. The boy was still in the room, looking as if he'd like nothing more than to disappear.

I walked swiftly down the hallway, keeping my eyes on the ground.

What on earth had happened to me? I had just backed out of a confrontation without defending myself at all. For perhaps the first time in my life, I had failed to stand my ground. What would Ariana say? I thought myself a coward. Such a thing would *never* happen again, I promised myself.

A coward. I couldn't be a coward. The true cowards were criminals, hiding behind their tough exteriors. A chill ran through my veins. That would mean I was on the same level as Moriarty. No. Absolutely not. There was little to no merit in the concept of moral absolutism. All faults were not equal.

I inhaled sharply and shook my head furiously.

Get a hold of yourself. You were just afraid to admit to Holmes what you'd told Andrew. Ariana would have said not to seek help and then lash out at anyone offering it.

But Ariana wasn't here.

Still furious with myself, I briskly strode down the stairs, following the same path Andrew had led me along not too long ago.

I was surrounded by people. I couldn't think.

I couldn't breathe.

Finally, I saw the doors appear in front of me. Pushing through, I found myself outside. Careful not to take in too much of the stench, I refilled my lungs a few times, gathering my bearings. In the end, I decided to walk around the area to clear my head.

I hadn't even made it to the end of Whitehall Road when the footsteps behind me made me pause. They belonged to someone exceptionally tall and thin, running – no doubt trying to catch up to me.

'Holmes,' I said calmly, my hands at my sides.

'Emily, what the hell is going on?' he asked, his cold grey eyes betraying that this was more than a serious inquiry.

It was an interrogation.

I sighed, preparing to tell him some version of the truth.

'I met Andrew when I was waiting in the Commissioner's Office two days ago. Yesterday, he was at the crime scene.'

At this point, I noticed that Holmes' lips tightened, as if he was thinking that the Commissioner's son had had no right to be there. I ignored him.

'He was there when I received the note from Moriarty, so he is partially informed of the matter now.'

I said nothing about the fact that I had told Andrew of my own free will, nor that he was completely informed. Holmes did not need to know that.

'Andrew Lynch cannot be trusted. He's a child, a spoiled brat coddled by his father. He has no idea of the true value of truth and fidelity.'

Holmes was wrong. Andrew couldn't hurt a fly. And he wanted to help me. I trusted the detective, of course, but he didn't know everything.

'I'm sorry, but you're wrong.' Without another word, I turned and walked away. Away from Holmes. Away from Scotland Yard. Away from the mess I had entangled myself in.

It began to rain. The cold drops hit me, making me shiver. But it made no difference.

I slowed my pace just long enough to glance back. The streets were clearing substantially because of the rain, and Holmes was nowhere to be seen. Shivering again, I bowed my head and continued walking.

An unbidden tear slid down my cheek. If anyone saw, they would not be able to distinguish it from the raindrops.

I do not know how long I'd walked before finally looking up at my surroundings. Although it was undoubtedly still daylight, everything was much darker. I could not see the sky at all. The rain was still falling.

And the stench… It was far, far worse than it was in other parts of the city. The odour of unwashed bodies and rudely dumped waste was everywhere. Rather than cleansing the streets of the permeating redolence, the water cascading from the sky was making it even more unbearable.

There was no doubt that I had found myself in the East End slums, where most London's crime originated.

Penniless women, turned out of the workhouse with nowhere to go, resorted to prostitution for a meagre source of income. Impoverished families turned out, or, worse, killed their children in order to have fewer mouths to feed. Drunken, jobless husbands returned home late every night to beat their wives beyond recognition. Yet this place was where the police force opted to send the fewest patrollers.

I considered asking someone for directions to the nearest train station or cabstand, but the characters roaming about seemed to be of the most unsavoury kind. Men in threadbare waistcoats and hole-riddled shoes lounged against walls, smoking homemade cigarettes or chewing on toothpicks. One man standing near an alleyway entrance was doing something most unmentionable to a woman in a shockingly low-cut dress.

I was rooted to the spot, hunching my shoulders and shrinking back into the shadows, hoping to make myself invisible. Finally, a constable in a dark, silver-buttoned coat and heavy boots rounded the corner.

Cautiously, I stepped out of the shadows and approached him. 'Excuse me, Constable, I was walking from Whitehall and I'm afraid I lost track of my surroundings. Could you tell me how I could get to the nearest cabstand?'

The constable looked me up and down in surprise. 'Now, what's a respectable young lady like yerself doing all alone over here on Gower Street?'

I blushed. 'Exactly what I said, sir.'

He sighed. 'The Commercial Road's just up this way.' He gestured with his thumb. 'I'll tell ya what: my patrol's about to take me up there. Why don't you let me escort you? No one'll harm ya then.'

I accepted his offer with profuse thanks, and we set off at a brisk pace in a direction I believed might be north. When we arrived, it was still dingy, dim, and damp, but I was relieved to see more traffic on what appeared to be one of the main roads in eastern London.

'Let me call ya a cab,' offered the man.

'Oh, no. I'm sure I can manage. Thank you, though.'

I turned to head for the cabstand, but the constable grabbed a hold of my arm. 'I've seen things while walkin' my beat, Miss. Things so cruel they make my blood boil at the very thought. The least I can do is extend a helping hand to a respectable girl in need.'

He had a few precious silver coins pulled from his pocket; no doubt he had planned to use them to buy a glass of brandy and a bite to eat before finishing his shift.

'No, you can't... I have money...'

'Nonsense. Where are ya goin'?'

'Baker Street.'

Awestruck by the civility and compassion of this man, I watched, slack-jawed, as he strode over to the cabstand and spoke a few words to one of the cabbies before beckoning me over.

'Now, you see to it this lass gets there safe,' he warned the cabbie, waving his truncheon threateningly.

The wide-eyed cabbie nodded and clambered up in his seat.

Constable Smith, as his embroidered lapel identified him, opened the door for me.

I smiled gratefully as I stepped inside. 'Thank you, sir.'

He returned the smile. 'It was nothin', Miss. Perhaps we'll meet again.'

And as the cab drove off, I rather hoped he was right.

The rain had subsided when the cab dropped me off in Baker Street, just two houses down from 221. The flat's door was unlocked when I entered.

At once, Mrs Hudson was upon me, taking my sopping cloak and hat. 'Mr Holmes was here, but he left looking for you. Thought you'd ended up somewhere terrible – like the slums, heaven forbid!' She shuddered. 'I'll send off a telegraph to Scotland Yard, have one of the runners let him and the doctor know you're safe. That client of Mr Holmes's is waiting upstairs. I've sent up some tea. Have some to warm yourself, dear, you must be chilled to the bone!'

As the landlady fussed and puttered about, one detail stood out in my mind.

Mr Koval was here?

I dashed up the stairs to the sitting room.

But it was empty.

The tea tray was indeed on the table; a half-empty cup suggested that Ivanov's aide had been here, but it appeared that he had left very suddenly.

Beside the tea tray, a single piece of foolscap paper lay discarded:

6th September, 1887
West India Docks
You will deliver the sum of 10,000 pounds to a boat called the Old Buccaneer by half past five o'clock this evening in exchange for the safe return of Mr Ivanov. Come alone. Bring the money or rest assured you will die.
J.M.

Oh, no. Where on earth would Koval have gotten ten thousand pounds so quickly? He would've had to steal it – unless, of course, he didn't have it.

He was planning to go without the money.

Which meant, of course, that he would end up dead. And Ivanov would not be returned.

In all probability, the ransom price would rise even higher.

I glanced at the wall. It was exactly five o'clock.

I stuffed the note into my pocket and, thinking of a desperate situation, grabbed John's loaded revolver from his desk.

'When Holmes comes back,' I called out to Mrs Hudson, 'tell him to meet me at the West India Docks, there's a boat called the *Old Buccaneer.*'

The long-suffering landlady opened her mouth to protest, but I was already out the door and waving down a cab. I promised the driver an extra sovereign if he could get me to the docks in fifteen minutes. He looked at me as if I were asking him to take me to Avalon, but didn't object.

Even at the ridiculously fast speed, it was not fast enough for my satisfaction.

However, he informed me it had been fifteen minutes exactly as we pulled up to my destination. Too rushed to bother with the details, I handed the man his extra sovereign. Then I bolted down the slick wooden piers.

Finally, I saw it. So small; hardly more than a sailboat.

The Old Buccaneer appeared to be deserted.

All I could do was wait. Crouching behind a pyramid stack of large barrels, I carefully drew the gun. It was then that I realised that it was my first time holding a firearm. I glanced at it curiously, studying its different parts. It seemed simple. I would disengage the safety lock, aim at my target and press my finger down on the trigger. It couldn't be any more complicated than archery, at which I excelled.

Peering through the stack of containers, I saw that this stretch of the dock was still empty of anyone worth noticing.

Then again, anyone Moriarty had placed at the scene was unlikely to attract attention until it was too late.

I wasn't sure how much time had passed, but eventually I saw Holmes and John dash onto the scene, looking about wildly. My brother was weaponless, looking none too pleased about it.

I raised my head just above the barrels to beckon them.

Within seconds, all three of us were pressed together behind a single stack of shipments.

'What in heaven's name are we doing here?' hissed Holmes. 'And why do you have Watson's revolver?'

John groaned. 'That's where it went. Give that here!'

'I got back to Baker Street and was told by Mrs Hudson that Koval was waiting upstairs. I went up to see him, but he was already gone. He had left this on the table.' I pulled out the crumpled note and handed it over to Holmes, reluctantly giving my brother's gun back as well.

'The imbecile is going to get himself killed!' muttered the detective, handing the note to his companion.

'Holmes, it's five-thirty exactly.'

We all peered anxiously through the dim haze. A lone figure was climbing onto the boat, empty handed.

Holmes stood and poised his own weapon. 'Koval, stop!'

Before the young and supposedly intelligent diplomatic aide could react, the tinkling of broken glass came from above us and Koval fell forward. There had been no sound of a gunshot, but dark and sticky blood spilled from the back of the man's head and spread onto the deck.

John clambered onto the boat, kneeling and turning the man over. 'Holmes, he's dead.'

In that single moment, I saw the great detective look weak for the first time. He sighed and closed his eyes, pinching the bridge of his nose with two fingers.

A pit dropped in my stomach. It was as though the air had been stolen from my lungs.

Although it had been no fault of his own, Sherlock Holmes's client had died. The look on his face was one of defeat.

Chapter 10: Come like Shadows

> *'Show his eyes, and grieve his heart;*
> *Come like shadows, so depart.'*
> *– William Shakespeare*

If the sun had indeed been in the sky when I arrived at the docks, it had long since disappeared. The temperature was rapidly dropping as the evening wore on. Shivering, I swept my gaze over my second crime scene in as many days.

Inspector Lestrade stood at the edge of the pier with Holmes at his side. John was a couple of feet away, interjecting into Holmes' statements whenever he felt the need.

Inspector Gregson, who had interviewed me at the hotel, peered over the body, writing in his notebook.

I had already given a sergeant, who had identified himself as Collins, my statement. Now I slumped against the wall of the warehouse behind the pier, watching the proceedings. The scene was in chaos, but as an eyewitness, I had no trouble seeing what had occurred.

Moriarty had placed a man in the warehouse window in case anyone interfered with the plan. When Koval appeared empty-handed, he carried out his kill order.

The real mystery was what kind of deadly silent weapon he had used.

Holmes and John both appeared rattled by this fact, but I had encountered such circumstances twice before. I didn't know how to explain it any more than they did, yet my stepfather had died in the same way. So had Lambert, the concierge employee. All other concierge members and guests in the building had heard nothing but a horse trampling a dog outside.

It was more than a little disconcerting that I had only half of the pieces to the puzzle. I knew that there was a picture hiding just beyond my reach. No, it was more than disconcerting.

It made me angry.

Having nothing else to do, my eyes canvased the scene once more. That's when I saw someone new arriving.

From the look of his clothing, I guessed it was Chief Commissioner Lynch. My speculations were confirmed when I saw the silent, demure boy following him.

'I sincerely hope none of you have touched the body,' called the Commissioner in a stern, bellowing voice.

He swept past me to peer at Koval's lifeless form, but his son hung back. Gradually, Andrew drifted over to me. He didn't meet my gaze, nor did I attempt to meet his.

Finally, I had to break the silence between us.

'Andrew, I'm so sorry about earlier. I should have said something, and I shouldn't have left like that. I just—'

Andrew still didn't look at me. 'Just forget about it.'

'But I—'

This time his hard gaze pierced through me. 'I said forget it.'

I took an involuntary step back. 'All right. I'm... sorry.'

The boy ran his hands through his hair, taking a deep breath. 'I'm the one who should be apologising,' he said at last. 'I should have been more respectful to you.'

'I think I can forgive you,' I replied.

'And about this morning – I understand. I would have done the same thing in your place.'

I studied him for a moment. 'They're all jealous of you, aren't they?'

Slowly, Andrew nodded, looking as if it was the last subject he wanted to discuss. 'As much of a help to the Force as Holmes is, he's still an amateur. A mere consultant. I think he envies me because I've seen more official police scenes than him.

'And as for Lestrade... Before being promoted to inspector, he spent the majority of his career behind a desk. I may not have seen as many crime scenes as him quite yet, but I'm barely seventeen years of age. Because of my father, I'm treated as a part of the Force, even though I'm far from it.' His voice wavered for a moment, but he quickly cleared his throat as if it hadn't happened.

'I suppose you've seen a lot, then? For your age, that is?'

'You could say that.'

Andrew studied my features much as I had studied his.

'I already know I am correct in saying that you have, too,' he said pointedly.

I tightened my lips, trying not to concentrate on the memory of just yesterday, when I had lost control of my emotions and poured out nearly every circumstance of my life to him.

'And it's not just what you told me.'

Honestly, I wished he would stop before I cried.

'It's in your eyes. You're young, but your eyes are ancient. Yes, they still sparkle, but they speak of horrors the likes of which many have never imagined.'

The words hit me like a cold wave. I turned my head away, wiping a salty tear from my eye.

Pull it together.

When I turned back, Andrew was looking straight at me. 'You know you're allowed to cry, right?'

I shook my head vehemently. 'No, Andrew, I'm not. I am thoroughly ashamed of the way I opened up yesterday. I don't mean to be blunt, but I hardly know you.'

He shrugged. 'What would you like to know?'

I was surprised to discover that I had no questions to ask him. After all, it wasn't like our relationship was anything more than slightly friendly.

Andrew looked for a moment as if he were going to prompt me to speak, but then he grabbed my arm and pointed wordlessly, shock bristling from the rigidity of his shoulders.

My gaze followed his finger.

'Oh my God.'

On the side of the building to our left, two words were printed in white block letters: Canary Wharf.

But that was not what had attracted Andrew's attention.

A huge, blood-red X had been painted over top of the already existing words.

X marks the spot.

A chill ran through me. I had been present at the scene for at least two hours… I swore on my own life that the letter had not been there before.

We both stared at it for a moment before Andrew's mouth began to work again. 'Should we tell someone?'

I glanced at the pier and the boat. No one seemed to notice the dripping red X that had appeared on the wall without explanation. 'No. They all have far bigger things to worry about, and besides… I have a feeling that was left for me to find.'

I moved soundlessly towards the wall across the cordoned-off street, beckoning for Andrew to follow. He did so, still awestruck.

About halfway across the street, he stopped me. 'Emily, what if that's actually blood?'

I rolled my eyes. 'Andrew, really. It's not like I haven't seen human blood before. I *snuck into* my first crime scene, for goodness' sake. Now are you coming, or not?'

Anyone else would have thought that Andrew was the frightened one, but I knew better. He was being chivalrous.

He would learn, hopefully sooner rather than later, that this was unnecessary. I wanted a compatriot, not a gallant knight.

I reached the wall first. The paint – or whatever it was – dripped still. I boldly reached out and smeared some of the liquid onto my fingers. It was sticky and dark. I supposed it still could've been paint, until I lifted the fingers to my nose and sniffed. The smell was slightly metallic.

'It *is* blood.'

Andrew swallowed hard, pulling a handkerchief from his pocket. He handed it to me to wipe the blood off my fingers. As

I did so, the sensation made my skin crawl. *Whose blood was that?* Whether it was human or not, the substance had once run through a living, breathing creature.

Holding in a shiver, I turned back to the wall, tilting my head.

Now it just looked like a cross.

I straightened my head again. Why would it have been left here in the first place?

My eyes fell closed as I thought back to the last time I had seen an X like that.

'...The centre point of the X is London. Therefore, the so-called treasure we seek is here.'

My eyes flew open. I barely registered that Andrew was still beside me, arms crossed as if waiting for me to come up with something.

'Andrew, you're taller than me, can you see which brick is at the centre of the X?'

He nodded and peered up at it. 'Wait... It's loose!'

Triumph and excitement coursed through my veins. 'Can you reach it?'

'I...think...so.' He stood on tiptoes until he could just reach the brick in question. He grabbed onto it with his handkerchief, as the blood was still far too wet. He looked back at the wall cavity. 'There's something in there. I can't quite reach it.'

'What about one of those boxes?' I suggested, nodding at a stack of shipping crates nearby.

Andrew immediately moved to go get one. Judging from the ease with which he picked it up, the crate was empty. He set it down and agilely climbed on top. This time, the reach appeared much less strenuous. In a few seconds, he had a small cigarette case in his hand.

I confess that my hand was shaking slightly as I reached for it, and it took me a moment before I could open the tiny box.

Inside was a small scrap of paper, neatly folded, that read:

I have aroused your curiosity, haven't I? You will not be staying off this case as instructed, if I am correct in guessing. Perhaps you remember what I said to you and your sister about curious cats.

You will pay the price.

There was no signature, but it was obvious who it was from.

My eyes remained hard, my expression unreadable. This time, I repressed my emotions.

Yet Andrew could still read me like a book. 'Emily?'

I didn't answer. I continued to stare at the note in my hand.

Finally, he snatched it from me to read it for himself.

'You won't let me tell anyone, will you?'

I inclined my head and raised my eyebrows. 'Well, showing anyone would result in them knowing that I am on the case without permission. And we have definitely resolved not to do *that.*'

He sighed and handed me the paper back. 'Emily, he's threatening you. Don't you see that? If you tell someone, they can help protect you.'

'I can protect myself, thank you!'

'You know of martial arts, then?'

My cheeks flushed. 'No. But I'm rather a natural at archery, and I'm sure I could shoot if given a firearm.'

Andrew shook his head, looking unimpressed. 'Emily, there will be times when you will not have a gun on your person.

Or you might not be able to get to it in time. You need to be able to fight with your hands and feet.'

'Teach me.' The words were out before I could even form the thought. Strangely, though, it was my honest response.

Andrew took a step back, mystified. 'What?'

'I said, *teach me.*'

He stammered for a moment. 'All right. If you really want me to... I suppose I'd be willing...'

I wasn't sure if he was actually going to finish that thought, but if he was, he didn't get a chance. He suddenly started walking towards something behind me.

'Oi! This is a police scene, Miss, you can't be here.'

I turned to see a girl walking towards us. Even in the dim light of the flickering gas lamp, I could see that she was very close to my height, thin as a rail. She had buttercream hair, with a single freckle on her fair-skinned cheek.

I could also see that she was wearing clothes that were far too expensive for her to be from this part of the city.

She stopped and cocked her head at Andrew. 'You look a little young to be with the police. And if this is a crime scene, what is *she* doing here?'

Andrew's hands flew to his hips. 'Now, you see here. She has as much right to be here as I do. Now if you will please exit the crime scene—'

She held up her hand. 'I saw the man who painted that X.'

'You know that's not paint, right?' Andrew interjected, at the same moment I was trying to hush him.

The girl's thin eyebrows arched. 'Blood, then? How dreadful!' She shuddered in an exaggerated way that made me think this didn't bother her one bit.

'Miss...' I started.

'My name is Nicole Camberwell.'

'Miss Camberwell, can you describe the man to us?'

'I saw him walking over here from one of the buildings across the street. He had a brush and a bucket of that dreadful stuff. I saw him take out a penknife and carve a brick out of that wall, place something behind it, then put it back. Afterward, he took his brush and painted that thing on the wall with the blood.'

'Did you see what he looked like?' Andrew asked her, sounding rather professional. 'What he was wearing, perhaps?'

'Well, he had on a dark overcoat and a bowler hat. He was of medium height and his hair was dark. He was not large, but rather solidly built. I could see his silhouette when he turned. He had a crooked nose – broken at least twice, I'd say – with a square jaw and a moustache.'

I did not recognize the man, but it had most definitely been an agent of Moriarty's. Perhaps even the man who killed Koval?

Andrew and I exchanged glances. Once again, Moriarty had flaunted his reach of power by sending one of his men into my path. The action had been as quick as lightning, as silent as death.

And, like a gunshot spilling red all over my stepfather's study, the hotel employee's lounge, the *Old Buccaneer*'s deck, the blood had appeared without any warning.

Chapter 17: Where Laws End

'Unlimited power is apt to corrupt the minds of those who possess it; and this I know my lords, that where laws end, tyranny begins.'
– William Pitt

The afternoon following the incident at the docks, I was alone in the flat, save for the company of Mrs Hudson who was taking care of some papers downstairs.

I had been rather withdrawn all day, not even appearing for breakfast and lunch. After I was sure that the flat was empty, I crept into the sitting room, finding myself filled with dread. I hadn't been alone in the room since Moriarty had slithered his way in. When I looked at the sofa, all I saw was an abyssal gaze;

all I felt was malice. Searching for safety, I curled up in the armchair by the fire. The seat seemed rather intimidating at first, being usually occupied by Holmes, but I found that it was really quite comfortable, and afforded a very rewarding view of every part of the room.

Except for Andrew, I had not told a soul about the note. It was currently stuffed into an envelope of newspaper clippings inside my desk. Not forgotten, but certainly abhorred.

Looking around me from my new vantage point, I banished Moriarty from my mind. Several of the day's papers lay untouched on the table. I only needed to glance at the top one – the *Pall Mall Gazette* – to ascertain that all the periodicals would be buzzing with news of Koval's death and Ivanov's disappearance.

Publicity was exactly the opposite of what this investigation needed.

As I was about to walk back to my chair, the title of the paper sparked a thought in my mind. *Mycroft Holmes.*

Sherlock had not so much as mentioned his brother since we had been to see him. As a figure of power in the British Government, Mycroft surely knew the goings on of both foreign and domestic affairs.

On our way to his apartment in Pall Mall, Holmes had pointed out the Foreign Office building, where Mycroft worked – although he had an office with his name on it in nearly every government building.

What was stopping me from going to see him?

I descended the stairs and gave Mrs Hudson a brief explanation, mainly that I was going out and most likely would not return until late.

I donned my cloak, pulled the collar close around me and opened the door. A very familiar face was right outside, hand poised to knock. When it opened, he started and turned around, pretending to be walking in the opposite direction.

'Andrew, come back, please.'

The boy stopped in his tracks, but made no other move.

Sighing, I advanced towards him. 'What's going on?'

He looked over his shoulder at me, face partially in shadow. His eyes were gloomy. At first, it appeared that he wanted to tell me something, but he was silent.

Finally, he said, 'I can't do this right now, Emily. I have to go.'

I almost called after him, but he disappeared too quickly.

Can't do what?

He sounded as if I were the one who had approached him.

Shaking off my questions about the irregular attitude of Andrew Lynch, I called a cab to Whitehall.

Once at my destination, I tipped the cabbie and stood on the sidewalk, staring at the impressive building. The Foreign Office was regal in appearance, which I supposed was not all that shocking, considering that it housed a part of the British Government. Columns and archways were carved and moulded out of what appeared to be marble; the gleaming white stood out considerably from the surrounding street.

I took a breath and stepped through the doors, once again stopping to blink in surprise. It was certainly nothing akin to the other sights I'd seen in London. The floor was made up of a great number of large squares inside of which were several other, smaller squares filled with Greek designs. They were polished until they shone like a mirror. A grand staircase carpeted with royal red ascended upwards, branching off into other staircases that led to different parts of the upper floor, all of which was encircled by an ornately carved railing, giving the impression of an enormous balcony.

But the design of the interior of the building, while making me feel inescapably small, was not the reason for my shock.

It was the plants.

It was as if I had stepped out of the urban frenzy of London and into a jungle. Palm trees and particularly bushy flowering shrubs loomed overhead, making it rather hard to see the upper balcony. They must have all been potted, but the foliage was so dense that it was difficult to tell, and the incredibly large number of specimens made it a little hard to believe. Indeed, the full impression was altogether disconcerting. I half expected to hear the calls of wild birds and primates overhead.

Peering around me a bit, I located the Commissionaire's desk, flanked on either side by slim potted palm trees, and walked over to speak to the tall and lanky man who was slouched in his chair, reading the sensational front-page article of the Times: the ongoing investigation into Alexei Ivanov's disappearance.

'Excuse me, sir, can I inquire about an employee here?'

The man folded down his paper to look at me with eyes so dark they were almost black. 'One of the Civil Servants, you mean?'

'Yes, sir. He doesn't work here full-time. His name is Mycroft Holmes; would you know if he's in today?'

The military-uniformed man pulled over a large black logbook from across the desk to look. 'He's in his office until four o'clock today. Our secretary, Miss Dunn, will be pleased to show you up. Won't you, Idelle?'

At the sound of her name, a woman in her late twenties, who was filing books and encyclopaedias on an incredibly ornate bookshelf in the area behind the desk, turned toward us. She sported a round, smooth face, slightly freckled, and dull brown hair pulled up into a bun.

'Of course,' she spoke quietly. 'If you'll follow me, Miss.'

She crossed the threshold between the office and lobby, carved in Corinthian spirals and intricate designs, and beckoned me to follow her up the grand staircase.

I sucked in my breath as we walked under the faux canopy of leaves. It was a shock there was no warm tropical breeze.

The first story was much like the ground floor in appearance. The floor was polished to an impeccable sheen, the looming doorways made of deep mahogany, trimmed in sparkling white. The velvety red carpets were spaced evenly down the hallway, giving the perfect balance of royal red and the same pattern as the downstairs. It seemed very illogical that all this splendour could fit on the inside of a structure that, although large, was flanked by other formidable buildings on all sides.

The Government clearly believed in stretching the limits of imagination.

The secretary, Idelle Dunn, led me to the very end of the hallway on the right side. She knocked on the imposing door lightly, and waited for a response. After a few seconds, the boisterous voice of the elder Holmes brother answered:

'If this is Miss Dunn, bring in the biscuit tin, please.'

'Actually, Mr Holmes, I have a visitor to see you.'

I heard Mycroft sigh loudly. 'Can they come back? I already have a small meeting in progress, you know.'

'It's Emily Watson, Mr Holmes,' I called through the door. 'If you have a moment to spare, I need to speak to you.'

There was silence for a moment and then: 'Come in.'

Idelle Dunn opened the door and stood back so I could enter. 'I'll find you those biscuits, Mr Holmes,' she said, and left.

I'm not sure what I was expecting, given the proportions of the rest of the building, but the office was huge. Mycroft's desk was on the far side of the room, with a chair facing away from a large window that was at least two feet taller than me. A dozen massive bookcases lined the walls, and a settee and an armchair were positioned diagonally on either side of an oriental carpet across from the desk.

Did all of Mycroft's offices look like this?

There was a depression in the seat of the armchair, as though it had been recently occupied. As I looked around the spacious room, I saw that a man was standing with his back against the nearest bookcase to the door, swirling around a glass of amber liquid.

'Miss Watson. How did you know to find me here?'

'Your brother told me you had a position here, and that you divide your time between this and… various other positions. I didn't actually know you were here today; it was merely a hunch.'

The elder Holmes simply blinked at me.

I gestured at the tall, suited man by the bookcase. 'I am sorry, I did not realise you had any kind of business going on.'

The stout government official with the bulging waistcoat shook his head. 'It is nothing to worry about, Miss Watson. In fact, if I have conjectured accurately, you are here regarding the same matter as this man.'

As Mycroft spoke, the stranger stepped out of the shadows cast by the natural light from the window and the lamp overhead with such a calm and fluid motion that he seemed to blend in with the very air in the room. He held out his hand to me. 'Whom may I have the pleasure of addressing?'

'Emily Watson,' I answered politely, lifting my hand to be kissed as I had been taught.

He did so gently. 'Inspector Patterson.'

My eyebrows lifted. 'Of Scotland Yard?'

He laughed. 'Originally, yes. But officially, I am with the Detective Service of the Home Office. Mr Holmes is an old colleague. Is she here regarding *that*, Mycroft?'

'As I said, Pierre, *if* I have conjectured accurately. Have I, Miss Watson?'

I bit my lip. 'Yes, Mr Holmes. I am here about the Ivanov case, and, more importantly, its ties to Moriarty.'

No doubt Mycroft had reached out to other high-ranking officials who could surreptitiously get a handle on the situation.

'You see, Pierre? It is safe to say his name.'

Even with Mycroft's assurances, Patterson squirmed uncomfortably. 'How is it that she knows about *him*?'

Mycroft's eyebrows rose almost to his hairline. 'This is *Emily Watson,* Pierre.'

Patterson's eyes grew wide. 'Surely she's not—'

I knew far too well from whence he had heard my name. 'Sir Ashford's stepdaughter? I am.'

'My condolences.'

'Thank you, Inspector, for your sympathy.' I hoped my voice did not reveal my annoyance at being treated like a grieving widow.

'Surely you are feeling anger towards the, ah, man who has taken your stepfather from you?'

'Oh, I am feeling anger towards him, make no mistake about that. But it is for a different reason.'

The Inspector's eyes filled with understanding. 'Your sister. Of course. As far as the periodicals know, both of you went missing together and have not been seen since.'

That was news to me, although it was logical. They wouldn't have reason to suspect anything else.

'Am I to assume that Mr Holmes has explained to you the truth behind my stepfather's death?'

'I have,' Mycroft interjected. 'Now would you mind enlightening me as to why you are here?'

Staring at the ground, I took a breath before speaking. 'I was only wondering if you knew anything. I promised your brother that I would steer clear of Moriarty's involvement outside of the Ivanov case, and he has refused to speak to me of it since then.'

'Coming to me about it as a clandestine alternative is not *"steering clear"* of it, Miss Watson.'

He was right, of course.

'Will you agree to not tell him? I am only requesting an update on affairs, not a way into Moriarty's organisation.'

Mycroft tightened his lips, but finally agreed. 'All right. Inspector Patterson here has volunteered himself to find a contact who will be willing to serve as our informant from inside the syndicate. He already has several men in mind, do you not, Pierre?'

The inspector nodded, taking a sip. I eyed the amber substance, trying to deduce its identity.

Mycroft followed my gaze. 'Before we move further, can I get you anything to drink, Miss Watson? Coffee? Tea, perhaps? I would offer you some of that sherry, but...'

'No, Mr Holmes, I am fine. Pray, continue.'

Patterson spoke thoughtfully. 'As Mr Holmes has just said, I have in mind several men who would, should they accept, find it a most desirable position. All that would be required of them is to listen and report back to us. I am sure that the Magistrate would grant them reprieve for their cooperation.'

I nodded. It made sense to have petty criminals get in with Moriarty; he'd be more than willing to accept business from them.

'This is all well and good,' I said, directing my statement at Mycroft, 'but has any of this reached your brother?'

Holmes's brother began to look rather uncomfortable. 'I know that this is the last thing you want to hear, but Sherlock is only an amateur. He is hardly equipped to deal with a case of this magnitude. If anything can be done to help him, I will see to it that it happens, whether he approves it or not.'

The fact that he wasn't planning on telling Holmes about this made me angry. But what right did I have to act like this? I was the one who was disobeying Holmes's rules directly.

I looked at Patterson. 'You're from the Home Office?'

'I am.'

'So does the Home Secretary know about all of this? How about the Prime Minister?'

The look on Mycroft's face became even more pained. 'Miss Watson, everything that we know is non-existent as far as the government and police are concerned. We are dealing with a very influential man. He has friends in high places; we cannot trust anyone with that kind of authority. With the right words and the right price, anyone can be manipulated. If they hold a position of high importance, they can wave a proverbial wand and change what is seen by those beneath them.'

I understood perfectly. Anyone's trust could be bought. After all, power corrupts.

For a moment the three of us sat in silence, myself in particular, allowing the government official's words to soak in.

Suddenly, the door to the office opened slightly, revealing the petite figure of Miss Dunn. 'I have your biscuits, Mr Holmes.'

'Please set them on the desk, Miss Dunn.'

When she had done so, he immediately took one out, taking a bite, inadvertently shedding crumbs from the shortbread all over his tie. He looked up, seeing that the girl was still standing there, hands folded politely. 'Is there anything else, Miss Dunn?'

'Yes, sir. There was a note left for you at the Commissionaire's desk.' She produced a cream-coloured envelope from her pocket. From where I was standing, I could see it as it was handed to the recipient. The wax seal was bright red, for business correspondence.

Then my eyes fell on the handwriting on the front.

My heart stopped.

Mycroft didn't seem to recognise the slanted penmanship, and slit open the envelope, still chewing his biscuit. His eyes scanned the contents of the page and slowly set down the biscuit on his desk. 'You may go, Miss Dunn.'

As soon as the door was shut, the elder Holmes set the paper down on his desk and wiped off his shirt. 'It appears that we have quite the problem.'

Chapter 18: Best Laid Schemes

'The best laid schemes o' mice and men
Gang aft a-gley.'
– Robert Burns

'And you were going to alert me of this *when?*' Sherlock Holmes' tone was livid.

'I am telling you now!' His brother's eyes blazed. 'We needed someone with contacts.'

'Mycroft, I have contacts!'

'Who cannot keep themselves out of prison!'

'Perhaps they *could* if they were employed by a man with such sway!'

'May I interject?' Inspector Patterson stepped forward.

Mycroft massaged his temple. 'I would prefer it if you did not, Pierre.'

'But sir, you still have not told us what that letter says.'

Leaning against the far wall to the left of the door, Inspector Lestrade raised his eyebrows, appearing impressed that Patterson had dared to speak without Mycroft's blessing.

Holmes spread out his arms exasperatedly. 'Yes, why don't you share that with us. It is, after all, the reason that you summoned me here all the way from Chiswick.'

Mycroft sighed deeply and handed the letter to his brother, looking relieved to get the damned thing away from him. Holmes read it, appearing stunned.

'You're not going to do it, are you?'

The man clasped his hands on top of his abdomen. 'I do not have a choice.'

'Have a choice in what?' I said on behalf of Lestrade and Patterson, who were looking positively lost.

Holmes sighed. 'Moriarty has made another ransom demand. Twenty thousand pounds to be delivered to the Ship Tavern on Gate Street in Holborn tomorrow at noon. There is, however, one extra stipulation.'

Lestrade's left eyebrow rose dubiously. 'And that is what, precisely?'

Another heavy sigh. Holmes looked straight at me.

'Emily, he says you must deliver the ransom personally.'

I opened my mouth, but couldn't speak, for my stomach churned uncontrollably.

It made sense, for I rather think he liked me in some strange, perverse way. Perhaps it was the false familial connection.

Patterson spoke for me. 'Then why was the note delivered to Mycroft Holmes?'

'Because I am instructed to come up with the money.'

Mycroft's face was more sober than I'd ever seen it, which was saying something, as he appeared to be a very serious man.

'It seems he is fond of the idea of the government paying to keep the whole affair quiet.'

'Does this mean my involvement is allowed?'

'No, Emily, it is not.' Holmes' gaze was harsh.

'Then I will be forced to ignore your instructions.'

'What did you say?'

'I said that I refuse to stay away. A man's life is at stake. He could be killed if we don't follow Moriarty's demands. Just because he wants to extract me from that equation does not mean that we should ignore the importance of other lives.

'Who will mourn for me? I should not think anyone, for all those whom I have truly known are dead or in captivity. I would say all of you would mourn, but I do not aim to gratify myself. Ivanov, however, is an influential figure. If he dies or is not returned, a vicious war will erupt. Potentially thousands of lives will be lost and an entire two countries will mourn. Weigh the consequences, I beg you. Think of why we are here – for Queen and Country!'

I barely noticed that my voice had cracked. Silent tears were rolling down my cheeks. My emotional outburst, however, appeared to have quite the effect on the occupants of the room.

Holmes drew back. Mycroft's eyes were on the ground. Both Lestrade and Patterson were eyeing my body language.

'That settles that, I suppose,' I said, wiping my cheek dry with the back of my hand. No one spoke as I exited the office.

I had learned not to go walking through the streets to alleviate my frustration. All I needed was to stand alone in the hallway to compose myself. I crossed to the railing overlooking the floor below and looked pensively through the greenery.

Unfortunately, it was not very long before Lestrade slipped out the door and made straight for me. 'Miss Watson? Are you all right?'

I assumed a stiff and defiant posture. 'I am fine. I merely want priorities to be correctly judged in the present circumstance. I am sure that you understand.'

He sighed and ran a hand through his permanently ruffled hair. 'You know why Sherlock Holmes cares so much, don't you?'

'I can't say I've given it much thought.'

'Well, you should. None of us have ever seen him like this around a lady. The only reason he normally accepts clients of the fair sex is because your brother won't let him send them away.'

'Your previous statement implies that you know why he cares about me.'

Lestrade massaged the back of his neck uncomfortably. 'I think it would be better if you heard the truth from him.'

I almost laughed at the absurdity of his suggestion. 'Inspector Lestrade, can you honestly imagine Holmes being honest about that?'

He too was forced to break into a smile. 'I think I should wish to be there to see it. But I know that he will, someday. I also know that you are incredibly observant. You will see it with time.'

After thinking for a moment, I spoke again. 'Lestrade, I do understand that he is only concerned for me, but that does not change the sense of duty that I feel. I will not hesitate to put myself on the line if it helps us accomplish Ivanov's safe return.'

'Emily Watson,' Lestrade said after a while, 'if we ever overcome the social boundaries, let me be the first to say that Scotland Yard would be honoured to have you.'

I do not think that I managed to close my eyes on the night of 7th September. My mind was in chaos. I dared not spare a thought towards the kind of horrible visions my imagination would conjure were I to lay my head down for more than a second.

In lieu of resting, as I likely should have done, I paced my bedroom floor for the entire night, rearranging the books on my shelf and the few items on my desk multiple times in an attempt to calm myself. In between the sorting and pacing, I snuck increasingly paranoid glances out the window, expecting Moriarty's henchmen to be watching the flat. But every time, the street was devoid of unusual presence.

It took me until dawn to realise that no one was there.

At breakfast, I could not force myself to eat. I don't think that I was very nervous. I wasn't nauseous either. I merely was not in the mood for anything at all.

As it turned out, after I had retired to my bedchamber the night before, Holmes had told John that I was going to deliver the ransom. But from the attitude at the table, it appeared that he had not been informed of the exact reason. I cautiously raised my eyes briefly to look at my brother. Ever since I had entered the room, he had been staring at me as If I were insane. I knew from the way he shied away from Holmes that he had not backed down without a fight.

Neither of us spoke a word, although as John set down his fork, I could tell that his hands were shaking from the noise it made against the plate. His expression and the tensed muscles in his neck betrayed that no amount of military discipline could quell what he felt, whether it be from anger or fear, or, indeed, both. For I knew very well that every anger was rooted in fear.

As soon as Mrs Hudson took away the breakfast plates, my brother disappeared without a word.

After a long period of taut silence between Holmes and I, Lestrade and Inspector Patterson appeared, the former lugging a large bag full of banknotes.

'I don't even want to know where your brother acquired this money, Holmes.'

'Requisitioned it from government accounts, of course. Mycroft *is* the British Government, in certain terms of the phrase, Lestrade. I would never believe him to have taken illegal means to get the funds.'

'Don't forget that he is your brother.'

'As if I would dare.' The detective's voice dripped with sarcasm.

'Emily.' Lestrade turned to me. 'We have arranged an operation of sorts. Patterson will be sitting at the corner table of the pub. Holmes will be in disguise as the bartender – the real one has been temporarily relieved of his duties and is being held as an accomplice to a fictitious smuggler's ring. Meanwhile, I will be outside. When Moriarty – or, more likely, one of his men – approaches, I will enter the pub and give you a sign. You will conduct your business with them, hand them the money and we will then arrest them for kidnapping and collecting a ransom demand.'

'Hold on just a bloody moment,' interrupted Patterson. 'Is that really enough to ascertain that Moriarty is behind the kidnapping? Where's the proof that it's him?'

'I've already taken care of that,' said Holmes, pulling a piece of paper from his pocket. He unfolded it to reveal that it was actually two pieces. One was the note that Koval had discovered the morning of Ivanov's disappearance, while the other was the ransom note that Koval had followed to his death.

'A specific line from this eccentric rhyming scheme was particularly instructive. It said, "look for my name on my very own crest." If you hold these notes up to the light, you will see a watermark in the upper right-hand corner. Magnify it,' Holmes handed the note and a convex lens to Patterson, 'and on the upper edge of the mark, which is a coat of arms, you will see a name.'

The government official peered through the lens at the paper. 'Moriarty.'

No one was bothering to detail the specifics of this plan.

'Black Dog.' I said. Everyone in the room looked at me blankly. 'Oh, for God's sake. The sign! *Treasure Island* has been the tune Moriarty's been playing this whole time, so let's play along. Lestrade, when you come into the pub, you'll tell Holmes as the bartender that there's a Black Dog outside. It's innocuous enough, no one else will take any notice.'

'..That's from *Treasure Island*?' the inspector asked.

'Of course it is, or she wouldn't have mentioned it,' Holmes cried. 'But your brain isn't, clearly…'

Lestrade fixed him with a sharp glare before turning back to me. 'Fine. There's a Black Dog outside. Go put your disguise on, Holmes, and stop mouthing off.'

The man in question grumbled a bit about dim-witted detectives and imbecilic inspectors, but slouched off to his bedroom nonetheless.

Everything felt strange, as though time moved in slow motion and I was the only thing going at a normal pace. Before I knew it, we were getting out of the cab and taking our positions around the proximity of the Ship Tavern.

Holmes and Lestrade had already carried the bag of money into the building, placing it beneath the table I was to sit at. A few other men were lounging at tables in the pub; they gave me suspicious looks as I sat down.

Meanwhile, Patterson was already sitting at the table in the corner behind me.

I sat there, silently, trying to quell my nerves. Occasionally glancing behind me, I tried to meet Patterson's eye, but he was always looking in another direction.

After a few moments, I saw a familiar figure across the street and tensed in my chair. My insides filled with the sort of dread that only came from watching a catastrophe unfold and being able to do absolutely nothing about it.

What was he doing here?

It appeared that Lestrade saw him too, for he turned around and motioned for us to stay put while he handled the situation. The thin, lanky boy started to cross the street remarkably quickly, and the inspector rushed forward to stall him. I could gather from their stances that a shouting match ensued. Andrew Lynch eventually overpowered Lestrade, who pointed down the street and yelled 'Black Dog!' in a useless panic.

The Commissioner's son quickly reached the pub, taking a dubious look back at Lestrade's outburst. If he entered, he would compromise our carefully planned entrapment. Surely

Moriarty had planted someone to keep an eye on things. That was the entire point of the signal.

If Andrew approached me, they would be aware that there was a police presence and we would fail.

I stood up and ran towards the door. One of the men blocked my path; he was very large and very muscular.

Aware that my move towards the door had not been appreciated, Holmes and Patterson sprang into action, but it was soon obvious that we were outnumbered. Three more men stood up and engaged my companions in combat. I was caught in the middle of what would seem to an outsider to be a disorderly, drunken brawl. The last thing I saw was Lestrade pulling Andrew away and rushing in before a hand clamped over my mouth everything went black.

Chapter 19: The Play's the Thing

*'The play's the thing
Wherein I'll catch the conscience of the king.'
– William Shakespeare*

I opened my eyes and immediately wished to close them again. My head hurt like hell, and even though there was very little light, it seemed like far too much.

The pain from the rest of my body hit me all at once. My left shoulder ached incessantly. There was a sharp burning sensation near my chest. I concluded that at least one or two ribs were broken.

Gently licking my parched lips, I blearily peered around to try and deduce my location. Contrary to my expectations of a prison, having been apparently kidnapped, I was in a well-furnished and comfortably heated room. Yet, there was only one light – a small gas lamp in the far corner.

The most uncivil part of my situation was that I was tied to a wooden chair with a coarse rope. It was just like I'd read in my adventure books.

I tried to struggle but found that the knots were too tight. My ribs seared with a pain great enough to render me incapable of breathing.

A thought hit me then, horrible as the first wave of pain. Andrew. He might be in some kind of trouble.

And what about the others? What would Holmes tell John?

My mind went back to Andrew. How on earth had he known what was happening at the Ship Tavern? He did have ample investigative talent, I supposed, being the Commissioner's son.

Oh, God, I hoped he wouldn't do anything moronically chivalrous, like track down my captors...

Of course, his occasional stupidity was outweighed by his more frequent bursts of brilliance. But every part of it, every part of him, was—

Lord, was I just about to think the word *attractive*?

I tried to stop myself, but it was obvious. Every time that I saw and spoke to him, something stirred inside of me.

Could it really be romance?

My stomach squirmed at the thought.

My thoughts were interrupted by the door opening with a soft creak. When I whipped my head around to face the noise, I gasped, far more surprised than I should have been.

Professor Moriarty's arms were crossed, fingers tapping against his forearms in a pattern that looked familiar. 'Dear me,

Miss Watson, you have been mistreated. I thought I gave explicit instructions that you were not to be harmed while being brought here.'

'That would have been difficult,' I said with a wince. 'It was a setup. Holmes was there. As were two Scotland Yard officers.'

Moriarty leaned back his head and laughed. 'I suspected as much. That is why I didn't go myself. Of course, I wouldn't have had the time. I have been rather busy as of late.' He clucked his tongue. 'Dear, dear, it does appear that I can't trust you. That's not the way we're supposed to play the game. You're just a bit too trusting. If you keep it that way, you'll never get your sister back.'

A lump suddenly formed in my throat.

'Where is she?' I asked in a low voice, my hands curling into fists where they were tied behind my back.

'Oh, don't worry, she's safe,' said my foe, walking over to turn my chair around. He glanced at my extremities and grimaced. 'I'll have to call in a physician to tend to you. Wouldn't want that concussion and broken ribs going untreated.'

'Where is my sister?' I asked again, hoping to sound threatening.

Of course, I couldn't be much of a threat while tied to a chair.

Moriarty put a finger to his lips. 'Don't you worry about that.'

He had turned my chair to face a curtain on the opposite side of the room that I had not been able to study previously. The entire kidnapping scenario was quite annoying in that regard.

My father's murderer drew the curtain back, revealing a piece of glass in the wall. For a split second, I thought it was a mirror, for the girl on the other side of it was my spitting image.

The very same girl ran up to the glass, trying to get as close as possible, her mouth open in a scream. I could not hear her words.

'Ariana!' I screamed. I began to struggle against my bonds more ferociously than I had before. I did not care about the intense pain in my lungs anymore.

As I struggled, tears began to fall down my face.

'Ariana!'

But just as I could not hear her, my sobs and screams were distant waves that could never reach the other side of the glass.

I did not see Ariana again.

It had only been a day since, yet it gave me a sense of the most utter desperation that we were kept in the same building but I could not see or talk to her.

They kept me in the same room, untied. I was allowed a military-issued cot with a pillow and blanket to sleep on.

Maybe, just maybe, if my friends managed to find out where I was, they could rescue Ariana too. I longed for nothing more than to be with my sister again.

Moriarty had a physician come to inspect my wounds. He introduced himself as Doctor Hargrave. After an examination closely overseen by one of Moriarty's men – one whom I had never seen before – he diagnosed my injuries as a minor concussion and four broken ribs. After instructing the guard to turn his back, the doctor bandaged my ribs and gave me an analgesic, all the while asking repeatedly how I had sustained these injuries. He was eyeing the rope burns on my wrists suspiciously as well.

After all my medical needs had been tended to, the good doctor was undoubtedly paid off handsomely and sent away.

I now sat on my cot thinking about what Moriarty had said the previous night:

'*If you keep it that way, you'll never get your sister back.*'

In order to get her back, this villain would have to let me go. Was he planning to? Was this just another way to punish my curiosity? Another way to show Holmes how much force he could exert? And if he *was* planning on releasing me, I didn't know when that would be.

I needed to get out fast. But I needed outside help.

Think, think, think. Any detail. Anything.

Doctor Hargrave's black bag. The engravings on the handle. He was employed as a police surgeon. If I could only see him again, I could have him pass a message to Patterson or Lestrade.

But I couldn't do it right away. I needed to make sure of something.

I stood up, grimacing as I felt my broken ribs searing with pain, and began to pace the room. I stopped by the curtain that Moriarty had pulled back to reveal Ariana to me before. Hoping against hope that she would be there again, I pulled back the heavy drapery.

The room on the other side of the glass was empty.

I tapped on it.

Sealed.

Soundproof.

It echoed from only my room – it didn't give the well-rounded echo of having reached the other side as well.

I sighed, a million thoughts and ideas flying through my head all at once.

What time was it? Certainly after three.

Doctor Hargrave had come at two. The guard outside my door had informed me that Moriarty had requested for me to dine with him at five. *Joy of joys.*

I didn't look forward to the prospect of another meal with that snake of a man, but I would endure it, for it gave me a chance to put my plan in action.

Heaving another sigh and grimacing, I sat and waited.

At what must have been five in the evening, the door to my room opened, revealing a young man with flaming red hair in a tailored suit. I was taken aback at his appearance; he wasn't the sort that I had expected to work with Moriarty. Although, I had absolutely no idea what that type might be.

'Miss Emily Watson?' He offered a hand to help me up.

I winced as he supported my weight and helped me pull myself to my feet.

'I'm Fred,' the man said with a wide and charming smile.

'Fred…' I prompted, thinking it was strange that he hadn't given me a last name, as courteous as he was in all other respects.

The man tilted his head amusedly. 'Now, we all know better than to give last names out freely in my field of work, especially not to charming young ladies with police connections.'

I laughed, realising that I might as well play along. 'And what about simply charming young ladies?'

'Well, they can sometimes pose an exception.'

'I suppose I'm right in saying that you've gotten far enough in your field, whatever it might be. That smile could get you anywhere.'

'It does have its perks, that I can say at least.'

We were walking down a long hallway. It was lavishly decorated, more so than I would have expected, considering the room that had been turned into my prison.

'This is quite the… establishment, Fred,' I said, looking around. 'How did Mr Moriarty afford to rent out this place on a whim?'

'The same way he can afford to keep my service and that of hundreds of other agents. The same way he paid off that doctor.'

I couldn't help but analyse his speech and the quality of his voice. 'You don't sound – or dress, for that matter – like the others. Where did Moriarty find a respectable collegiate such as yourself?'

Fred laughed again – a lyrical, baritone sound that fit right in with his smile. 'If I told you that, we'd both be in deep, deep waters. Let's step away from those and enjoy our dinner, shall we?'

There was an open doorway at the end of the corridor. Through it, I could see a large, elaborately decorated room that could have been repurposed as a ballroom. Perhaps that's what it was. A table was set up in the middle, around which three men were seated: Moriarty, a lean and haggard man with uneven stubble and hard eyes and a tall, imposing man with dark hair, a receding hairline and a long, straight nose. The last man's eyes were grey and piercing, and his suit seemed even finer than Fred's.

As the young man pulled out a chair for me, I eyed the third man, wheels turning in my head. 'And you are Mr Ivanov, I presume?'

He looked up in surprise. 'How did you know?'

'The quality of your clothing and the fact that you look far too uncomfortable here to be one of Mr Moriarty's men.'

'That's *Professor* Moriarty to you,' said the despicable creature. Without looking, I could feel his repulsive beady eyes boring into me.

I turned my gaze and gave him a look. 'Don't try to kid yourself.'

Fred sat down beside me and averted his eyes.

I noticed that a roast chicken and platter of potatoes were in the middle of the table.

Moriarty picked up his fork. 'Well, then, I suggest we eat.'

Throughout dinner, my tormentor and the other man were conversing in low tones. Try as I might, I could not make out any of what they were saying. Suddenly, the man looked up and fixed me with a gaze so piercing that I immediately looked away.

When we were finished eating, Moriarty turned to me. 'I am glad to see you are faring well, Miss Watson. If you behave yourself, we shall do this again tomorrow. I may even have a surprise for you.'

He nodded at Fred, who stood to escort me to my room.

Now. This might be my only chance.

As Fred helped me stand, I gave out a cry and collapsed to the ground. My escort knelt, easing me onto my back. At the same time, the remaining men at the table stood up in alarm.

As I worked to make my breathing seem as heavy and pained as possible, Moriarty beckoned to the young man kneeling beside me. He went over to his employer, and I heard them speaking softly.

'Should we send another doctor? We could pay him off, just like the other one.'

'No. That's far more trouble than it's worth.' Moriarty cast a glance in my direction, his eyes emotionless as always.

'Stay here with her. I'll send for Hargrave again. Mr Ivanov, follow me.'

He then swept out of the room, the Russian delegate too frightened to do anything but follow in his wake. The third man did not even need an order to follow obediently after his master.

Fred swiftly knelt beside me again.

'You're a doctor,' I said weakly, through my intentionally laboured breathing. 'So why go to the trouble of calling in someone from the outside? You don't need more liabilities.'

He shook his head as he shrugged off his jacket, rolling it up. He slid it under my head to support my neck. 'Not for quite a few more years yet. I'm certainly not qualified enough and Mr Moriarty does value the safety of those he keeps close for his own purposes. Now, don't talk. Save your breath.'

I chuckled, making sure to punctuate it with a grimace. 'You called him Mr Moriarty.'

'Yes, now hush, and for God's sake, *breathe.*'

I followed his instructions, closing my eyes and concentrating on my breaths. To Fred, it would seem that my efforts were focused on continuing to breathe, but in reality, they were focused on making my breathing seem as unstable as possible. For good measure, I cried out loudly and curled in on myself.

Fortunately for my charade, the pain soon became real, for I could feel my bandages cutting into my skin with my movements, and tears began to run down my face. Fred took a firm but gentle hold of my shoulder and pushed me back onto the ground.

'Stay on your back now. The doctor should be here soon.'

He was right. A few short moments later, yet another man with whom I had not been acquainted showed a ruffled Doctor Hargrave into the room. I wondered how on earth he had gotten here so fast. He had to live very close to come on such short notice.

The doctor knelt beside me and opened his bag.

Fred stood behind him. 'Should we move her?'

Doctor Hargrave looked at him sharply. 'Heavens, no!'

The medical student nodded and continued standing there a moment before Hargrave shooed him with a hand.

'I will require privacy, my good sir. An examination of the wounds will require the removal of certain garments. I must ask for you to leave.'

Fred quickly complied with the physician's instructions, closing the door behind him.

Once the door was securely closed, Hargrave spoke in an even tone. 'Miss Watson, you may stop faking a collapsed lung now.'

I stopped my heavy breathing and looked up at the man, blinking a few times before finding words. 'How did you ascertain so quickly?'

'The pallor of your face, Miss Watson. You are nowhere near pale enough. In fact, you are more flushed from the effort of maintaining an irregular breathing pattern.'

Rather sheepish, I sat up and grimaced.

'Truthfully, Doctor,' I said quietly with a glance towards the door, hoping no one outside could hear us, 'I only needed an excuse to get you back here. I noticed the engraving on your bag earlier. You're a police surgeon with the Mets.'

He stiffened. 'What bearing does that have?'

'You might have guessed that I was not brought here of my own free will, or for shelter, or protection, or whatever cock-and-bull story they fed you. It may also have crossed your mind that there is only one reason they could have a need to pay you off. And I do know you were bribed into silence, but please. I need you to pass a message to Scotland Yard. They never have to know it was you. You'll be safe. I promise.'

Hargrave looked leery, but said nothing. In a moment, he whispered, 'And to whom am I passing the message?'

'Inspector G. Lestrade. Tell him to get Holmes and John and Patterson as soon as he can.'

We both snuck wary glances at the door.

Hargrave bit his lip, but nodded. 'All right. Consider it done this very evening.' He collected his bag and offered me a hand up. 'Come on, now. Take it easy. You still shouldn't be moving about with those broken ribs.'

He supported me over to the door and opened it. Moriarty, Fred, and the man who had shown the doctor in stood waiting in the hallway.

'She'll live. But make sure she sleeps well tonight and is cautious with how she moves for about a week.'

Moriarty nodded and motioned to Fred. 'Take her back to her room.' He turned to the other of his men. 'Show the good doctor out.'

Fred took my arm to support me as we began the walk back to the room with the single gas lamp and my simple little cot, all the while inquiring how I was, if I was sure I was fine.

'Yes,' I reassured him every time.

When we reached my room, Fred let me in and closed the door on his way out. I sank onto my cot without any desire to sleep.

Chapter 20: Love is Then Our Duty

'Youth's the season made for joys,
Love is then our duty.'
– John Gay

Hours later, probably closer to ten o'clock, the door of my room opened and a figure in a long coat appeared. He turned up the gas lamp to improve visibility.

I jumped up and cursed so profoundly that he winced.

'Holy mother of hell, Andrew Lynch! What in the name of Christ are you doing here?'

'I was there when Doctor Hargrave passed the message along and I insisted upon tagging along. Good work, by the way. Oh, and I really should teach you martial arts. With a knowledge of self-defence, you might never have gotten yourself into this mess.'

'Where are the others? How did you get in?'

'Searching the building for Ivanov and your sister. We got in by posing as guards. The man at the front door, daft type. He just assumed that we were new recruits and let us right in.'

Suddenly there were voices down the hallway. Several men were running in our direction. Andrew swore softly and flung the door closed, bolting it. He glanced around urgently.

'All right, you've been here longer than me. How do we get out? Think fast. They look stronger than the door.'

I cast a hurried look around the room before realising. I rushed over to the curtain and pulled it back.

'Can you break through this?'

Andrew scanned the room for something to use and quickly picked up the chair which I had been tied to the previous night.

'Stand back,' he advised.

As I took a couple generous steps back, he rammed the window. The glass shattered as two of the chair legs broke off.

Moriarty's men pounded at the door, which was bursting at the hinges. Andrew was right. It wouldn't hold long.

I looked at the broken window. Shards of glass still stuck up from the bottom edge. How would either of us get over it?

Andrew caught my gaze. 'Do you trust me?'

'What?'

'Do you trust me?' he repeated, looking into my eyes with the most honest gaze I had ever known.

And at that moment, I knew the answer.

'Yes.'

With a hint of a smile on his lips, Andrew put his hands on my waist and lifted me up.

'Tuck your legs in,' he said, and I obeyed. He swung me over the dangerously sharp edges of the window.

I landed safely on the other side, stumbling slightly, but still on my feet.

Andrew took off his coat and laid it over the shards, using it as a cushion while he jumped over nimbly. As soon as he made it into the room where I had seen Ariana, the door gave way.

'Go, go!'

The men fired several shots. We threw the door open and made our escape into a hallway.

'Left or right?' Andrew gasped.

'I don't know,' I managed through the white hot pain spreading through my chest cavity.

More shouting. The men were coming from the left.

Andrew grabbed my arm. 'Let's go right.'

There were stairs leading downwards. At the bottom was a door. A cold breeze seeped from under it.

We were so close.

More shots were fired. All of them missed. But then the door opened.

Another man joined in the hail of bullets.

One of the shots sounded different.

Andrew fell to the ground.

I immediately dropped to his side. Blood was pouring from a spot on his left shoulder.

'No, no, no.'

The boy blinked, grasping my hand as tightly as he could. 'Emily, I should tell you what I was going to say in my father's office the other day.'

I shook my head. Tears blurred my vision. 'It can wait. Just hold on.'

He grasped my hand tighter and my heart skipped a beat.

'No, Emily, it can't. I… I may be falling in love with you.'

I didn't know what to do.

Andrew cried out loudly, then went limp. His hand fell from my grasp and his head rolled to the side.

No.

He wasn't dead.

He couldn't be dead.

It was just a shoulder wound.

'John!' I screamed. 'John!'

I looked up to see the shooters running in the opposite direction. Two familiar faces, which I was so glad to see, had run through the door, ready to shoot anyone who dared to oppose them.

Lestrade took one look at Andrew's body and bolted back down the stairs. 'Doctor!'

A second later, John flew up the staircase two by two. He pushed me back. I was too much in shock to object.

My brother quickly felt Andrew's neck for a pulse. He then ripped off his jacket, applying pressure to the bullet wound.

'Lestrade, get Emily to the cab. Patterson, come help me move him.'

The inspector assisted me in getting up. I obediently followed him, though I had no idea what was happening.

My vision was slow and disjointed. Everyone's voices came from far away. My breaths were ragged, wet gasps. My head hurt like hell and my chest felt as though it were on fire.

I felt the cold night air hit my face. Lestrade guided me to wherever it was we were going.

Home.

Home would be nice.

I had a longing for Thorndon Hall again.

Or was my home Baker Street now? I wasn't sure.

I didn't feel sure of anything, in fact.

My mind registered one thing: my sister was not outside waiting for me. I saw a man with dark hair who was slightly balding, whom I dimly recognized as Ivanov from the dinner table.

My twin was not there.

'Where's Ariana?'

My voice sounded slurred, wet, distorted. I wasn't quite sure if I was coherent.

Holmes put a hand on my shoulder. 'We searched the whole building. Moriarty and your sister were both gone. All that was left were a few air guns, German imports, which are being collected as we speak. I am sorry, Emily.'

What was he saying?

The pain in my chest was too much. My mind was a balloon, floating away.

The world became even more disjointed.

I vaguely tasted something warm, metallic. I thought I'd opened my mouth, but no air was moving in or out. Everything dimmed, then blackened.

※

I woke up to closed curtains, but I could still see light through them. Feeling far too groggy and sore, I could only blink as everything came into focus.

My brother was sitting in my desk chair, now pulled over by my bed, presumably for him to keep watch.

Keep watch over what?

Then memories rushed back at me. The kidnapping. My sister. Andrew. Collapsing outside of Moriarty's building.

I tried to pull myself up into a sitting position. The motion was greeted by a burning sensation and a great deal of dizziness.

John gently pushed me back down onto the bed with his left hand while taking hold of my wrist with his right. He timed my pulse against his pocket watch for a minute.

'How do you feel?' he asked softly.

'It hurts.'

'Well, that means that you're alive, which at present is the best we could hope for.'

'What happened?' I asked, relaxing my shoulders against the soft pillows. Raising a hand to massage my throbbing forehead.

'Does your head hurt?'

I nodded, the movement making the pain even worse.

'When the sedatives completely wear off, I'll give you something for the pain.'

'You still haven't answered me.'

'One of your broken ribs punctured your right lung,' my brother, the doctor, explained. 'You collapsed on the street as Patterson and I were carrying Andrew out. I had no choice but to drain the fluid right there or else you'd have been too far gone.'

I grimaced. 'Funny, I feigned the same thing to get Hargrave back. Wait, Andrew! Where is he? Oh, my God, please tell me he's—'

John put up a hand to quiet me. 'The boy is fine, Emily. He lost a lot of blood, but he's just fine. When I left him less than an hour ago to come sit with you, he was awake.'

'I'm going to see him.' I started to sit up again. Once again, I was firmly pushed back down.

'You suffered a punctured lung and were near death only last night. You aren't going anywhere.'

'How long are you going to force me to stay in bed?' I groaned.

'At least another two days.'

'What about Andrew? Can he come visit me?'

'If he's strong enough to rise without fainting by later.'

'Hand me *The Republic* from my bookshelf.'

John raised his eyebrows. 'Not *Treasure Island?*'

'I don't know if I'll ever be able to read that book again. Plato, if you please.'

My brother fetched the requested tome and left me in peace with my classics. I immediately put the book down. Of course, I couldn't focus on reading at present, and certainly not on Plato.

My mind was buzzing with what Andrew had said right before falling unconscious. What exactly did it mean? And more importantly: did I feel the same way?

Late in the afternoon, my thoughts had finally quieted enough for me to read. I was immersed in philosophy when a soft knock came from my door. I looked over and saw Andrew standing there, his left shoulder bandaged, his arm in a sling.

'How are you feeling?' I asked, resisting the urge to spill out the things I had been thinking about all afternoon.

'I was about to ask you the same thing.'

I shrugged, setting my book on my nightstand. 'John said I'll live.'

Andrew nodded and sat down gingerly on the edge of my bed. 'As will I.'

He opened his mouth to say something else, but before he could, John walked in. 'Mr Lynch, your father telegraphed and requested your immediate presence at his office, should I deem you strong enough.'

'And do you?'

'Yes, but I want you back here daily to examine your shoulder.'

Andrew smiled and stood, his smile quickly becoming a grimace. He tipped an imaginary hat at me. 'Duty calls. I expect it won't be too much longer before you see me again, Miss Emily Watson.'

And as he left the room, I turned my face away from John and smiled to myself. Love, affection, and the whole romantic lot wasn't a concept that I was well acquainted with.
But I certainly didn't mind an introduction.

Three Days Later

Scotland Yard's lobby was as bustling as ever. Petty thieves were escorted in and out of offices. Inspectors and secretaries hurried to and fro, collecting files and transporting evidence.

From where we were, I could see a wooden board with grainy police photographs of a dead body and the crime scene around it. A name sat at the top in a neat print: Sally Billings.

I looked at Holmes who was looking in the same place.

'Absurdly simple,' he scoffed. 'A displeased customer.'

Judging from Holmes' words and the low-cut dress Sally Billings had been wearing, I gathered that she must have been one of the Unfortunates for whom prostitution was the only means of survival. Even that was a risk hardly worth taking. I knew well enough from reading the papers that the ladies of the night made up a disturbingly high percentage of all murder victims, making it by far the most dangerous occupation in London.

Lestrade jogged up to where the three of us were standing.

'Alexei Ivanov is travelling back to St. Petersburg today. Hopefully his native government has a better idea of what to do with him than we do.'

'He'll need a new political aide as well,' I added grimly, recalling the cool evening at the docks where Dmitri Koval had met his untimely end.

'If he makes his way back into politics,' Holmes said. 'As my brother has informed us, the Russian government has caught wind of Ivanov's ties to revolutionary groups here in London. There is a good possibility that he might spend the rest of his life in prison on suspicion of treason.'

'That is not the only thing I'm here to tell you,' said Lestrade solemnly. 'Doctor James Hargrave didn't come in this morning. I must tell you, he's far too punctual – if you can fault a man for that. I sent a man to his home to make sure everything was all right. The news he came back with is grim. Hargrave is dead. A gunshot to the back of the head. My man talked to all the surrounding neighbours, but no one saw or heard a thing.'

We all stood in shocked silence. Lestrade didn't need to explain anything else to us. It was evident that Moriarty had caught up with the doctor and he had paid the price for carrying my message.

The man who had been so crucial to my rescue was dead.
Because of something I had asked him to do.
A knot formed in my stomach.

I swallowed hard, forcing my mind onto another plane. I could think about this all I wanted later. Not right now, in the middle of the crowded lobby of the Metropolitan Police.

Before anything else could be said on the topic, Andrew strode briskly across the room, grimacing as the movement jarred his slinged shoulder.

'Inspector, Doctor, Mr Holmes. My father asked if you could see him in his office.'

My brother turned to me as Holmes and Lestrade headed for the stairs. 'Stay here. And *don't* get kidnapped.'

And thus Andrew and I were left behind. We stood there awkwardly for a moment before he put his right hand on my shoulder.

'Emily… I'm sorry for what I said the other night… Before…' He gestured to his injured shoulder. Unable to maintain eye contact, the boy looked at the ground. 'I just didn't know if I would…'

'Live or die?' I finished for him softly.

He averted his eyes and nodded. 'I know it must have taken you by surprise, especially considering the situation. I'm sorry about that.'

'Don't apologise for your feelings.' I gave him a rueful smile. 'It is true that it took me by surprise. But I've been thinking about it for a few days and I've decided that… I really don't mind.'

Oh, damn, I messed that up.

I had meant to say that I felt the same way.

May my subconscious suffer eternal damnation.

Andrew Lynch laughed. 'Does that mean what I think it does?'

Glad that my intentions hadn't been misunderstood, I laughed too.

'Yes.'

He grinned lopsidedly at me, a wayward strand of hair falling in his face.

'So, then. How about those martial arts lessons we've been talking about? I know a corner of the archive room full of decades-old case files that no one ever needs.'

'Are you sure you can, with your shoulder like that?' I cocked my head playfully.

He shrugged, grimacing as if he'd forgotten that minute detail. 'I'll figure something out. I promise,' he added hastily, catching a glimpse of the stern look in my eyes.

'Very well then,' I said, a small smile twitching at the corners of my mouth. 'Show me the way, Mr Andrew Lynch.'

The boy who loved me grasped my hand and led me through the throngs of officers to a small door in the back corner of the room. Upon opening it, he gestured with a sweep of his arm.

'After you, Miss Emily Watson.'